Haunting The Cape Fear Coast

Thirteen Ghostly Legends
From Wilmington And Beyond

Joe Sledge

Books By Joe Sledge

Did You See That? A Travel Guide To North Carolina's
Out Of The Ordinary Attractions

Did You See That? On The Outer Banks

Did You See That? Too!

Did You See That Ghost?

Haunting The Outer Banks

In The Shadows Of The Pines

Haunting The Carolina Coast

The Unmerciful Sea

(As John Martell)

Bess Truly And Her Zap-Gun Rangers

Republished, as Editor and additional material

Nag's Head; Or, Two Months Among The Bankers

Kinnakeet Adventure

Haunting The Cape Fear Coast

Thirteen Ghostly Legends
From Wilmington And Beyond

Joe Sledge

For Callie

Table Of Contents

Introduction

Wilmington was my first vacation. I think that's why it seems so special to me. My parents first took us to a campsite where we pitched a big tent for my brothers and me, along with my mother and father. I must have been about three years old, wild eyed I'm sure at this new place I was seeing for the first time. It's funny how living at the beach  meant that seeing a full on forest of standing trees, along with a pond and geese bigger than me caused the same reaction of wonder and amazement that most people from inland probably had the first time they would see an empty and open shore, with the Atlantic Ocean stretching farther than they could see.

I don't remember much of the trip. I remember chasing the geese. If I only knew then about those geese what I know now! I know my mom gave up sleeping on a sleeping bag and went to the station wagon. Now that I'm a parent, and older, I can't blame her. What I really remember, only in pieces, I admit, but very vibrant pieces, is the next day when we went to the *USS North Carolina*.

The Battleship North Carolina was enormous in the eyes of a three year old boy. It bristled with cannons and guns. It towered higher than any pine tree I had ever seen. It was mine to explore.

I was too little to really run around; the deck and all that was part of the ship were certainly not meant for a little kid, and tripping hazards abounded, but still, I loved it. I don't know how they got a plane on there.

And the alligator! There was an alligator that showed up in the marsh right next to the battleship. We had heard about the alligator for weeks before we went, and I really wanted to see one. What kid didn't? I guess now alligators are a common sight around the the golf courses and waterways of the area, but back then, for a three year old, well, that was a real prize.

Like I said, I was too little for the ship. The big anti-aircraft guns had to be cranked by my brothers, and I couldn't run down the ladders like my Navy veteran father. But none of that mattered. I had a great time.

And with that, Wilmington sucked me in. It was a magical place. I wouldn't get back for nearly thirty years, and yes, the place changed, of course, but so had I. I still loved the place, with all the differences from my beach, or even California, where I was living at the time. It was an old city, with history in the grand buildings and all the stories there were inside them.

It would take even longer for me to learn all, okay, not all, but a lot, of the events of the area, how important it was and still is. I discovered that there are a lot of ghost stories there, the place is ripe with spirits. Far from having to search to find thirteen tales, I had my pick of them. I always try to search out stories that maybe even the locals may not know, and because of that I didn't include some of the usual chestnuts, including the ghosts of the *North Carolina*. I'll explain more of that in the Afterword. Right now I just want to enjoy these tales. I hope you become as big a fan of the area as I've become.

J.S. -June 2023

Bellamy Mansion

Wilmington

"It gets a little weird at night."

That understatement would not be fully understood until much later on when Becca Thatch was done with her visit to Bellamy Mansion. It was late, later than the usual tours would go through. Even though it was a dark and cold January evening outside, enough light still illuminated the grandiose mansion from inside and out. Streetlights filtered through the windows that graced the front of the statuesque antebellum home. From the inside, a mix of period style lighting added a soft warmth to the rooms.

Becca already knew that Bellamy Mansion was more than a "little weird." She was on an evening tour, hosted by her long time friend, Carrie Harper, who was a volunteer docent at the mansion. Carrie had been able to get Becca to come for an uncommon evening visit, as the mansion, now run by Preservation North Carolina, usually closed at 5:00.

"So, you mean weirder than normal?" Becca asked as they closed the door behind them to the main entry.

They had already toured the outbuilding, a smaller two story house that matched the mansion in some ways, while in others it was profoundly different. The smaller building to the northeast was the preserved quarters for the enslaved people that the Bellamy family kept at their home.

Carrie had explained the history earlier, outside in the cold.

The Bellamy Mansion had been built by the desire and need of Dr. John Bellamy, who was a merchant and physician who parlayed his businesses into becoming not only the wealthiest man in the state, but one of the wealthiest in the country at the time. He married and had children, eight with the ninth on the way, and realized that his Wilmington townhome and other residences just wouldn't fit in with the growing family. In 1859, be began the construction of what would become Bellamy Mansion. The three story building would have a sunny south facing kitchen, fancy living and visiting areas, and a small but warm upper floor for the children to stay. The architects also added a belvedere to the roof. The belvedere, Latin for "beautiful view," was actually meant to capture the cooler open breezes at height and bring the refreshing air into the house to cool it on Wilmington's hot summer days.

Dr. Bellamy and his wife benefited from their enslaved workforce. The architects designed a small house in the back of the estate to house the nine household workers kept there. Bellamy's major workforce of over a hundred enslaved people fared no better, working at his plantation fields and tar turpentine plant. The household workers included at least three young girls, the daughters of enslaved women, who were forced to work as personal "maids" to Mrs. Bellamy.

When Becca had first entered the small quarters for the enslaved people, she had immediately shuddered. It was cold and still, as well as dark. The dark creeped in upon her, almost as if a haze was enveloping her eyes. She had felt slightly nauseated and had to lean on the wall to hold herself up. "This place…' was all she could say before she slowly tumbled out of the gloom into the backyard, lit by a soft but comforting brown light of the streetlamps nearby.

"Are you sure you want to see this?" asked Carrie as they had gone up the steps to the mansion.

The reason Carrie asked was that when Becca was younger she had studied the bits and pieces of history from her Wilmington home town. She focused on the local people, ones that seemed to appear and disappear without making a mark in any book, but to her they were still important. She had noticed slowly that she had begun to feel for them. Becca felt their emotions and desires. She began to understand who they were, even though the people were long gone and forgotten to time. It had taken several years for her to realize that she had, reluctantly, become empathic to the lives of people long ago.

"I mean," continued Carrie, "with your…" she almost touched her head with a swirling finger.

Becca frowned. She didn't like anyone insinuating that she was "psychic." Or that she was crazy.

"No, I'm fine, it doesn't bother me much. I think the slave quarters just caught me off guard. That's a sad place."

Once inside the mansion, Carrie told the rest of the history. The home was finished in 1861, but Bellamy and his family were barely able to move in before having to leave due to a terrible yellow fever outbreak in the city. They escaped to their home outside the town at a time when Wilmington had become a hotbed of disease and danger, as the Civil War had just raised its ugly head to their coast as well. By the time Wilmington had fallen, Bellamy Mansion had become the home to Union General Joseph Hawley and his wife. Dr. Bellamy and his wife Eliza, both staunch secessionists and supporters of the Confederacy, as well as slaveholders, were not pleased to have General Hawley in the home that they had barely used. Eliza met with General Joseph Hawley and his wife, Harriet. Dr. Bellamy was none too kind to the occupying general who lived in his house. Eliza was reportedly cool and precise, but inwardly winced at being fed figs from what she perceived as her own tree. It would take an act from President Andrew Johnson for Dr. Bellamy to finally regain his home.

"Only some of his family got married and had children. The last person to live here was his daughter, Ellen Bellamy, who died here in 1946, at 93," Carrie ended her often repeated lecture, but this time added, "She seemed to harbor her father's anger right up until she died. And maybe even afterwards."

Becca looked at her friend quizzically. "What do you mean?"

"Come upstairs, I'll tell you, and you'll see." Carrie led her up the grand staircase.

The second floor had an open landing that looked out over the front garden. Becca looked around, trying to find the reason for a feeling of discomfort. Or more likely hate. And judgement.

"The story is, Ellen Bellamy still haunts this place," Carrie pointed toward an old wheelchair, which seemed to detract from the decoration rather than add to it. "That's her wheelchair. Other docents have told me that they have found it moved from place to place on the floor, but I haven't actually seen that myself."

Becca was skeptical, too. She didn't know much about ghosts, but she knew that a lot of what people thought they saw could be explained away pretty easily. Still, there definitely was something or someone there who was, Becca thought for the right word… "Prickly."

Yes, that was definitely it. If it was Ellen Bellamy, the feeling was that she was prickly, like a cactus. She was unhappy about having people in her house, but she couldn't come right out and show it. And that made her even more "prickly."

"Over the decades, people have seen the shadow of a woman up here. Some say she appears in that doorway, but when you walk over after her, there's no one in the room," Carrie pointed toward one of the upstairs rooms. "And of course, there have been sightings of a figure in the window, seen from the outside. But that could easily have been a trick of the light," Carrie supposed. She had never seen, heard, nor felt anything in her time in the mansion.

"But, I gotta tell you, Becca, sometimes, this place does feel a little creepy," she acquiesced. "And I'm not the only one who says so.

"Let me take you up to the third floor." Carrie led her friend toward the steps for the top of the house. "This is where it gets a little weird," she warned.

As they walked up the stairs, the house changed. Gone were the wide rooms and tall ceilings. The panels were of warm dark wood, with fewer windows. The rooms were small. "This is where the children's rooms were," Carrie explained. "When we get up here on tours, people kind of freak out a little. They all get edgy, and want to leave. They are ready to get up to the belvedere and the beautiful view. Even though there's less room up there."

Becca was only half listening. She snapped out of her thoughts, and answered her friend. "Well, there you go. This floor is tight, small, and no big windows. It's not meant for adults; it was built for kids. Everyone is just getting claustro…"

Becca stopped talking and froze. Carrie looked at her.

"Did you hear that?" Becca asked.

"What?" Carrie was already moving into the "little weird" part of how the house made people feel. Seeing her friend just stop and freeze at a sound only Becca could hear was unnerving.

Becca put up her hand to shush her friend. For a moment, nothing happened. Then, the two felt a soft *thump*, like the wind had blown a gust up against the house. But outside the trees were still,unmoving.

"What was *that*?" Carrie asked. "It felt like someone jumping onto the floor."

Becca was still listening. "Do you hear that?"

Carrie heard nothing but the beating of her heart, getting louder and faster in her ear every moment. "No. What do you hear?"

"It's like… laughing."

Becca heard it more clearly now. It was definitely the sounds of children laughing and playing. Again the floor shook softly, like a child jumping from a bed. Carrie felt the tremor, but heard nothing. Becca spoke again, saying, "I bet whoever was underneath these rooms didn't really like all that bouncing around." At the moment of her thought, the back of her neck got warm and sharp.

Prickly.

Carrie was noticing something, too. The rooms were closing in on her, in her imagination. She knew that Becca was feeling like something was going on, which was only made worse because Carrie couldn't feel what Becca felt. Carrie had a sudden urge to get out of the third floor. "C'mon," she grabbed Becca's wrist and fairly pulled her up to the belvedere. "I need a little air."

At the top of the house was the belvedere, the "Beautiful View." The small covered parapet had twelve windows all around, affording a view of the entire city from four stories up. Even though the windows were closed to the winter cold, Carrie felt a comfortable relief of just having an open view, and to be out of the confines of the third floor. It took her a moment to catch her breath, not entirely due to the climb.

They stood quietly for a minute, just enjoying the view. Far off the lights of downtown almost hummed with life, and the Cape Fear flowed past that, with the spotlights of the USS North Carolina battleship even farther away. Wilmington was an old city, with lots of ghost stories. "And lots of other stories, too," thought Becca. She knew her home had a long history, for good and bad.

She thought about what she felt and heard on the floor below, then spoke, with measured words, even though it was only the two of them in the belvedere. "Tell me something," she asked Carrie, "was Ellen Bellamy a bit like her father?"

"What do you mean?" asked Carrie.

Becca looked down at her arms, resting on the windowsill, then glanced at her friend's, doing the same thing. "You know, was she... *like* him?"

"Yes.

"Some people think that Ellen is still here, as a ghost, because she doesn't like people being in her house. She gets mad and tries to take it out on people. Certain people more than others."

"Well, she's definitely in a different world than when she was alive, that's for sure," commented Becca. "But it really does feel like she's mad about who comes in the house. I just don't think it is the visitors, though."

"What do you mean?"

"Were there any kids that lived in the slave quarters?" Becca asked.

"Yeah," Carrie responded, "There were three little girls, and a baby or toddler. We don't know much about her. "Why?"

Becca wasn't sure how to explain it to her friend. People rarely took the description of these psychological phenomenons well. Even though Carrie was her friend, and an old friend at that, it was just hard to get another person to understand.

"I think," her voice broke a little, and she cleared her throat, "I think that... Look, sometimes, it's not a ghost."

"I know that, girl," agreed Carrie.

"No, wait, you don't understand," Becca got a little perturbed by Carrie interrupting. "It's more than that. It's... It's..." she stammered at trying to explain.

"Hey, I'm sorry," Carrie said quietly. "I shouldn't have interrupted you. Just say it. After tonight, it's not like I'm not going to believe you." She made a vague notion of what had happened to them downstairs.

"Okay," Becca *humphed* out a breathy sigh. "Sometimes, it's not a ghost, but more like a memory. Like, the past is let through to the present, or trapped, no, that's not it, like it's written in the ether of life, here, in a place that had an important meaning.

"The laughter, the voices I heard downstairs, those weren't the kids of the Bellamy family. I think it was the daughters of the enslaved people that had to work here. Like, when they were young, they played with the kids upstairs, until they could be forced into work. Did the Bellamy children ever play with the other kids?"

"We, well, I don't know, I mean, maybe," Carrie never thought of that.

Becca continued, "How would you like it, being born into that, at first just being a kid, not seeing a difference, then slowly, you are forced out of being a little girl into being a slave for the same people you once played with? Seeing it all happen. Then seeing everything change? I bet the families of the former enslaved people stayed here after the Civil War, didn't they?"

Carrie nodded. "For a few months. The general was a noted Abolitionist who did a lot of work to get the emancipated to become freeplanters and get an education, I know that. They probably all left when the Bellamy family came back. Why would they want to stay?" Carrie commented derisively.

"Well, I think that the children of former slaves are up here, jumping from the bed and laughing, while the ghost of Ellen Bellamy fumes from down below, unable to do anything about it."

Carrie opened her eyes wide in the relative dark of the belvedere. "You mean there are ghosts of kids up here?" She wasn't sure how she felt about that.

"No," Becca insisted. "Not ghosts. It's memories. It's the past. I think that Ellen Bellamy is still steaming about what happened to her family home, and she's remaining here, angry, miserable, and taking out all her misery on anyone she doesn't like. But she's the one bringing all her own pain. She may not have even experienced it, but she knows, she *just knows*," Becca used an insistent tone of someone confident in their thoughts despite everything being a lie, "that those kids ran through *her house*, but all she can do is glare and stew in her wheelchair. Maybe that thing does move around, with her ghost pushing it back and forth in bitterness, just wishing she could run over those kids upstairs.

"And until she lets all that go, she'll be here, trapped, forever." Becca finished.

The two stood silently for a moment, high up over the house. "Okay…" Carrie finally spoke, "I'm not looking forward to it, but lets go down and get out of here."

Becca could see that her friend was clearly shaken, and agreed quietly that they would head outside. The stairs were a very small obstacle as the two raced quickly down through the top two floors and made their way out the front door.

Becca stood in the garden out front. Carrie had to lock the doors and turn on the security system, so she stayed on the front porch as she fumbled with the locks and codes.

In the quiet still air, Becca heard Carrie curse softly as she put in the code incorrectly. "Rats!" was her only whispered blasphemy. Becca could tell that Carrie had indeed been rattled by the events of the night, as well as Becca's testimony. She decided that they would discuss more pleasant things on the way home, or perhaps have a long stop somewhere downtown. Yes, the less said the better.

Becca looked up at the mansion, with its glowing soft lights gleaming inside, and the hazy glare of streetlights on the outside. For a moment, she glanced at the second floor window. There, in the soft yellow light, she saw the outline of a woman, gray and translucent, as if she sat just beside the sill, as only her head and shoulders were visible. Shocked, Becca was immediately distracted by the same shadows on the third floor. Only these were smaller, and seemed to move more freely. From far above, Becca wasn't sure if it was her imagination, but she swore she heard the sounds of children laughing.

As she looked back at the second floor, the gray shape had disappeared into smoke and nothing.

"Definitely *not* going to mention that," Becca thought wisely, as her friend walked down the steps toward her.

Spirits On The Cape Fear

Cape Fear River
Christmas, 1892

Christmas Eve brought no presents to the people of Wilmington on a bitterly cold day. Only snow and biting wind came forth from a blinding storm that sent anyone that had a home indoors to listen to the gusts howl down chimneys in demonic songs. The fires were well stoked in an attempt to keep the cold at bay. Few residents were successful, but they still counted their blessings, as those with no other place to go suffered a far worse fate over the three days the storm held its icy grip on the port city and neighboring towns.

The suffering did not stop at the water's edge. Ships were caught in the gale. They often ended up crushed and splintered on unseen shores with ropes and masts tangled into a macabre display. It was unknown if the crews and passengers were more fortunate to have been lost into the cold sea or broken upon the shore. The coast guard found that they could do nothing to aid those in distress. When the rescue boats went out, those at the stern found they could not see their shipmates at the bow, as the icy blizzard was too thick for their sight.

But time, tide, and travails held no sway with Captain John W. Harper. He was the skipper and master of his ship, the two deck mailboat *Wilmington*. She would sail under any circumstance, as long as she had power, no matter what the sky and the pounding Cape Fear threw at her. He was both master and servant to the ship. What he said goes, but the mailboat always had to go.

Unless it was hampered by a small rivet. One of a thousand that held the boiler together, the little bolt had given way, cracking the big boiler and releasing pressure to the point that the *Wilmington* was stranded in the Cape Fear River. Embarrassed, and mad, the captain's baby face visage of smooth soft skin hid his sailor's anger well, but less so the multitude of expletives he let forth, stunning most of the passengers aboard who all clutched at their Christmas packages they planned to take home to spots along the Cape Fear all the way to Southport.

With the aid of a slow but dependable tugboat, the *Wilmington* was brought to dock at her namesake city while repairs could be made. The bulk of the passengers exited for warmer quarters, as the repairs would take well into the night, and the engineer seemed to have an even fouler mouth than the captain.

All but one of the passengers disembarked, with only Mr. McMillan remaining aboard.

Captain Harper, with little to do and no distractions from the other passengers, was happy for a more erudite distraction in the form of the former blockade runner of Mr. McMillan. His tales were much more pleasant entertainment than watching the poor drunks stumble out of the waterfront pubs into the snow. They had shared their tales of how the Scots settled in North Carolina after a tempestuous life of oppression and war in their home in Britain. McMillan was able to supply a more personal story, as his surname would expect.

"Do you know of the British garrison and old prison barge that once sat at Orton?" Mr. McMillan asked. "It would have been in 1781."

Captain Harper stated he had no knowledge of it, but was intrigued by the introduction of this tale.

"It not only is part of the treachery and terrors of war, at the hands of the British occupiers, but has personal meaning to me," began Mr. McMillan, "for my very great-grandfather was held there, to be executed along with two other Scots, before escaping." McMillan told the entire tale as they awaited to sail.

McMillan's grandfather, a Scot who had been sent to the American colonies as an outcast, had settled in Hillsboro. He was found and captured by a British officer, Colonel David Fanning, who proceeded to take his many prisoners on a march back to Wilmington, home to the British loyalists and Governor Burke. His grandfather and two others were then taken to the garrison near the remains of Southport, and placed aboard the rotting and salted prison ship.

After several attempted escapes, the three men were pulled from the barge, given sham trials, and ordered to be executed. Only by the fortune of lot did the other men go first, as they were tied to a tree, then shot by a reluctant group of British soldiers, for even they had no desire to shoot unarmed men who were bound. The two fell where they stood, not even removed before McMillan's great-grandfather was dragged forward.

Even in his condition, wasted from starvation on the barge, the man still had fight in him. He smote one guard in the head, knocking the man senseless at his feet, and then threw the other as the English soldier tried to wrestle him to the ground.

Even with the sights of a dozen muskets upon him, his great-grandfather seemed to dodge every shot fired at him, piercing his clothes but not one entering his body. He disappeared into the woods, with the enemy under no desire to chase him. He fairly ran all the way home, a distance of over seventy miles, and lived not only to tell the tale, but a score longer than his less fortunate compatriots.

"Some say," ended Mr. McMillan with a note of conspiracy and delight, "that the other two Scots still walk about, or row a phantom boat in the water, in search of ships to take them back across the Atlantic, to their ancestral home."

It was a gloomy story, certainly, but one which ultimately had a happy ending, Captain Harper pointed out.

Captain Harper then was given notice that the boiler was fixed. The *Wilmington* would begin her trip, now repaired, under the weather of a still raging snow and a dark, clouded sky. Omens and portents swam in the icy wind.

"No, stay," commanded the Captain to Mr. McMillan as the *Wilmington* put out from the docks. His passenger had planned to go back down to the lower deck to ride out the trip alone, but the captain liked the companionship on a night when the visibility was measured in an arm's length. Having another sailor's eyes would do more good than harm, the Captain thought. Additionally, Captain Harper genuinely liked the older man.

"If you wish," politely responded Mr. McMillan.

Most of the crew laid belowdecks, huddled by the engine room, where the heat and steam would stave off any cold night, now that the boiler was sealed. Only Peter Jorgensen walked the bow, lead line in his calloused hands, constantly watching. The tide was going out, making shoaling more of a promise than a fear. "Three fathoms! Mark two! One and a half, she's shoaling fast, Cap'n!"

The warning came too late as the *Wilmington* stuck aground. Captain Harper cut engines, and with a gust of gale, his ship was pushed back into deeper water.

The sudden shift did nothing to increase the captain's confidence, nor Mr.McMillan's.

"I used to run my steamer to here during the unpleasantries," he used a delicate term for the Civil War. "Once I came under fire for twenty hours until my ship was shot out from under me. My entire crew was captured, and I barely escaped by swimming miles to shore in rough surf. I confess, that seems like a pleasant day compared to this. I have never seen such a storm."

"I fear we are drifting again," the captain tried to adjust the helm, "and the chains are now stuck!" A torrent of descriptions emanated from the captain's mouth, so much so that when done, he almost blushed and hid his face. Mr. McMillan only agreed with him with a nod, not judging the foul language harshly.

"We are out of the channel, Captain!" called Peter. "She's shoaling! We're on the jetty! Impact!" his warning was as loud as it was useless. The reinforced bow crushed into the soft wood of a jetty, and the *Wilmington* was again stranded.

With that, a contrite Captain Harper went forth to check for damage. He was ashamed, even though he had no right to be, that his ship was impaled upon the wooden jetty. The crew said nothing; they knew to keep their mouths shut.

With the ship stranded for the next six hours, as the only way to free the *Wilmington* would be a rising tide, the crew hid belowdecks against the cruel weather. Ony Peter Jorgensen, the mate, still walked the decks, keeping an eye out for passing ships or danger. He could barely see his hand at the end of an outstretched arm. Peter found his mind wandering. The tall Dane thought of the cold but calm Christmases of time passed. Only when an icy wind bit into him through his heavy coat, did he stir and turn against the wind.

When he did, he saw a sight that struck him colder than any frozen gale. Standing on the deck, no more than six feet from him, stood a man in rough torn clothes, all dripping wet and shivering cold. Peter called out to the man, "Who are you?! How did you get here?!"

The figure said nothing. He only shook from the cold, as one hand held the rail, while the other pointed a bony and stiff finger toward the tall hill of Big Sugar Loaf, just inland of Carolina Beach.

"Are you mad?" called Peter. With no answer, he reached out to the man, only to see him vanish into the snowy ether.

Moments later, he stumbled in shock onto the wheelhouse, white with fright. "I have seen… a ghost!"

Captain Harper, a grave and intelligent man, immediately took Jorgensen to have been drinking on duty. "This man is drunk!" he accused.

"I am not drunk!" answered Peter. His voice was terrified, but stone sober. "I just saw the visage of a man on the deck. When I reached for him, he disappeared!"

Captain Harper immediately ordered the ship to be searched. Clearly a man had somehow come aboard from a wreck, possibly a lifeboat or a piece of wreckage, and had to be found. The crew searched every corner of the *Wilmington* with hot burning safety lamps, looking into every corner and over all the gunwhales.

"Clearly the man has some supernatural cause for his insistence," said Mr. McMillan. "As a Scot myself, I am familiar that there are things beyond our comprehension on the far side of the spirit world."

After searching and finding no one but themselves, Captain Harper went back to the wheelhouse, where he found Jorgensen, still shaken, but still sober, drinking coffee at a seat.

"What did you see man? Did he try to talk to you?"

"I will tell you what I saw," insisted Peter. "If he spoke I heard nothing. But his face, the look he had on it, the way he gestured toward the Sugar Loaf… Captain, if you were at a point where you could do nothing to save the one person you loved, but there was someone who could, and all you could do was point and plead, sir, that would be the face I saw.

"I shall never forget that face."

"Perhaps you dreamed it," suggested the Captain.

"While holding a lamp, in that cold?" stammered Peter. He was so shaken he had no care for how he spoke.

"Did you know the man?"

"I have never seen the man before. And I hope to never again," Peter shivered.

"We are near the old town of Charlestowne," noted Mr. McMillan. "Perhaps we have been visited by a lost spirit from the ghost town."

"How is the tide, Mr. Jorgensen?" asked the captain. He was ready to steam far from this place and be done with ghosts.

"Rising for two hours now sir," Peter responded. "She's rising a little already."

"Let us plan to make way."

With that, Captain put his crew to new tasks, taking their minds off ghosts, even for a moment.

With the deepening water, the *Wilmington* finally freed herself from the jetty, with the damage being only to the wood pilings.

Captain Harper and crew would quickly begin to wish they were still stranded. The wind lessened, not significantly, but enough to thicken the snow around them. In the dark, strange shapes of sea birds trapped by the storm flew by in ghostly forms. Flashes of soft white appeared in the gray and black of night, like banshees circling the cursed ship.

Suddenly there was a crash, as a gull, blinded in the storm and darkness, crashed into the glass as it headed toward the light of the wheelhouse. The broken and bloodied bird lay lifeless at the captain's boot.

"A foul omen," commented McMillan. "I urge the greatest of caution. For I know of nothing else to offer." The old sailor looked at the younger, and both were ashened by the events. Captain Harper was comforted by the lights ashore now visible, as they passed the small colony of Lilliput, but McMillan cooled his confidence by pointing out that Admiral Frankland, a Royal Navy man, once owned the plantation, and his ghost was said to occasionally sail the waters nearby.

McMillan began to tell the story of how minutemen siezed the British palace nearby, now just ruins, when they heard a foul shriek carried on the wind.

Immediately, McMillan went silent and ran to the deck. The cry was definitely human, and as much so a sound of sheer terror. The waves pounded the bow, splashing McMillan with a freezing wall of water. He wiped his eyes, but took no other mind.

A blast from the ship's whistle sent Jorgensen running to the wheelhouse. "Did you hear a call?" asked Captain Harper.

"Aye, I did," answered Jorgensen.

Again, the call came, high pitched and terrified. "All stop!" ordered the Captain. The boat ended all forward movement, but bobbed like a cork in the unstable Cape Fear. "Crew on deck!" came his next order, and the entire crew rose from the warmth with intensity. No sailor would let any weather, no matter how foul, keep them from any form of rescue. Captain Harper sent out three quick blasts of his steamer whistle.

"It came from over there!" directed Jorgensen, "near the Sugar Loaf!"

"Could it be an animal?" asked McMillan.

"That hill is barren of life, a sand hill with no seed kind enough to take root, let alone an animal. That is the call of a man."

"We can not send our boat into this," Peter gestured into the darkness.

"Have the men stand by on all rails with casting lines," ordered Captain Harper.

The crew stood at the ready, nervous with every wail on the wind. With nowhere to run, and the captain at their backs, they attempted to stand tall during their distress. Many shivered, and not from the cold.

Peter Jorgensen jumped with fright, letting out a cry, as an icy hand fell upon his shoulder. It was only Mr. Platt, the engineer, who pointed with a startled inquiry, "Look! Over there!"

In the snowy mists came an outline of a decrepit barge, all black and rotted, as it bounced roughly in the high waves. "Captain, about two cable lengths to port!"

But Captain Harper had already seen it. The strange worm eaten barge exuded no sound, no oars plied the water. He ordered ahead dead slow, to keep the *Wilmington* from shoaling again, as they crept toward the hulk. Looking at Mr. McMillan, he showed his own fear in his eyes, for the barge glowed phosphorescent in the misty haze of night. "You know more of these things than I," he said, "and it seems all the ghosts have come out with you on this night."

McMillan responded, "They could be mortal men on that thing, in need." It was all the prompt the captain needed to remind him of his duty, even on a night as this.

"Stand by to heave to and throw a line!" he ordered.

The *Wilmington* churned slowly toward the ghostly craft, like a hunting dog following down its prey, knowing what it chased was wounded and ready to bite. Waves picked up the ugly barge, now close enough to view in the grave lights of the ship. The crew of the *Wilmington* saw clearly the barnacles and rotted splinters on the deck.

The barge rose on a wave, almost tossed into the deck of the mailboat, and the crew saw clearly for the first time the men aboard. Two creatures, pathetic and drawn, sat on the big raft. They were dressed only in tartan rags, the remains of their Scottish garb. Their ankles were bound in heavy chains and their wrists were bound and bloodied by salt rimed ropes. Their faces pleaded a silent call of help, as the two sat, their hands raised above them, as if in a begging prayer.

Peter, stunned at first from the sight, immediately shook off his fear and threw his line. The rope passed clearly over the barge, with the line easily falling onto the laps of the two shipwrecked souls.

Only, the line passed cleanly though the men and the rotted barge. In seconds, the craft melted into the salted air and snow, even the glow wisping away into snowflakes and dust.

Immediately, the shriek happened again. Captain Harper said nothing, but increased speed. No one spoke for a few moments, as no one knew what to say.

"Starboard! Hard a-starboard! Captain, we are running down a wreck!" Peter called out a warning.

Captain Harper spun the wheel, narrowly avoiding a ship cracked open and capsized. On the splintered hull, two men clung for dear life. With delicate skill, Captain Harper came alongside to cast a line to the men and have them brought aboard.

As the first climbed over the gunwhale, Peter held a lamp to the poor man's face. "Captain! This is the man I saw when we were stuck on the jetty!"

Mr. McMillan quickly realized the events of the night. "His spirit was almost lost. It found its way to the nearest point of rescue, coming to this ship in his last moments."

The two rescued men explained that they had been bound to Wilmington from the Bahamas and were caught in the gale. They stayed with the ship while the other crew tried to find their way to shore on lashed spars, but they had been torn apart in the churning sea.

"Have you ever seen Wilmington before?" asked Captain Harper.

"No, sir," said one. "I was unconscious for a time, and I dreamed I saw a steamship coming to save us, but I never saw the land, nor any of you," he stared directly at Peter Jorgensen, who was a complete stranger to his eyes.

With the rescued men warmed and fed, stowed belowdecks, the *Wilmington* continued its trip to home at Southport. The sun had finally found its way through a cracked sky. The storm began to abate, and the temperature rose, as did the barometer. By the time the *Wilmington* docked, the rolling waves had turned from hills to racing ponies, running up the river in regular patterns. Southport was covered in an icy snow.

Captain Harper walked in the quiet of the Christmas morning. The only sound at first was the crunch under his feet as his boots broke the icy loam. Then came the far off waves of Fort Fisher's beach, and finally, the birdsongs as he opened his gate. The notes mixed into an angel's song as the rough and tired captain made his way home, and saw his sleeping child, who had passed the night in peace, and would soon open his young eyes to the peace of a Christmas morn, knowing all was now right in his world.

29

The Cotton Exchange

Wilmington

Most old cities seem to have ghosts like they have mice. Plentiful in number, but their appearance often brings repulsion, disgust, and terror. Wilmington may have its share of spirits that lean toward the malevolent side, but this city benefits from a long time of sustained positive growth, and there are ghosts that seem to be pretty happy with the way things are going.

Take the Cotton Exchange, for example. Now it is a series of buildings that have been refurbished into shops and restaurants. Long ago, going back into the late 1800s, they were still just as successful. The Cotton Exchange was run by James Sprunt, a notable figure in Wilmington's past. The Cotton Exchange was just that, a business Sprunt ran that sold bulk cotton, a plentiful product in North Carolina that turned the fields snow white even in the warmth of early summer. Cotton was shipped from the bustling port to places across America, as well as across the Atlantic to England and the European continent.

That wasn't the only business to be run at the many buildings along what used to be Nutt Street, now North Front Street. The area had a plethora of businesses over time. Not only were there mills and retail stores, including a thriving Sears, Roebuck, and Co., but there were also services, from a large Chinese Laundromat, to a larger mariner's salon and brothel.

The buildings suffered when Wilmington had deteriorated as the Atlantic Coastline Railroad offices left for sunnier climates in Florida, starting around 1961. By the 1970s, the buildings were unused and targeted for demolition, as many others had already fallen to the wrecking ball. It was cheaper to tear down and build something new than it was to restore the large spaces.

Fortunately, a group saw the value of the buildings and saved them. In the process, they have made several ghosts very happy, as haunted activity of the Cotton Exchange has picked up with the growth of new shops in the complex. As old walls made of hand hewn wood from sailing ships were exposed in the renovation, so did the spirits reveal themselves as pleasant decorations from another time, happy to help out, or just participate in the experience.

In Top Toad, a girl likes to unfold the folded t-shirts, while another young girl was equally mischievous in The Scoop when it was open. She was known to play with the ice cream equipment.

Little kids must be a bit of theme for the area. A ghostly boy has been seen playing around the O'Brien

Building as well. Perhaps he got too much ice cream and is working off the ethereal energy from an otherworldly sugar rush.

The more stately ghosts certainly don't go for such playful antics, though. While the buildings may have stayed the same, in silhouette, since the 1880s or even longer, not everything has remained since then. The docks and waterfront have seen their share of hardworking sailors and laborers, but also Victorian era travelers in their finest clothes. A woman in a long dress, primly attired, has been seen wandering the shops and hallways. Perhaps she was an oceangoing traveler who intended to arrive in Wilmington, but sadly never made it off her ship alive. Her spirit was all that was left, and in her dignified way, she still found the ability to disembark. She now remains at the Cotton Exchange as a permanent guest who enjoys the shopping and sightseeing that she wanted to do over a hundred years ago.

On the other side of, well, the Other Side, is a guest of a different sort, but of a similar era. In Paddy's Hollow, a little hidden cache of a bar at the Cotton Exchange, a male ghost has been seen appearing in the mirrors as he wanders through the pub. He wears all black, including a tall top hat. He has even been seen walking through the bar and wall.

Obviously the soul is a spirit from another time, but little else is known about him. Locals refer to him as Fred, a moniker probably intended to lighten the fear of a ghost wandering around while you enjoy a cold beer. He may be just another Victorian era spook, happy to visit a bar even in his afterlife, just out enjoying the evening.

Though with his clothing, including fancy black top hat, he may have been associated with a nearby cemetery, now long gone. Unlike other graveyards where the dead have risen as ghosts to walk among the living, he may have worked there. His outfit is that of a caretaker, or possibly a professional pallbearer, dressed up to give those who passed on one more respectful trip to the ever after. And having to ever after carry the dead to their graves, who wouldn't want to stop off for a drink or two?

Regardless of who he was, or any of the spirits at the Cotton Exchange, one thing is for sure. There certainly are lots of ghosts there.

Emma Baldwin

Wilmington

Emma Mitchell wanted her name to mean something. She had been born into a good family, and wanted to keep up appearances. Marrying a successful dentist, who also had a good name, would certainly help her with that.

She had fallen in love with Dr. Andrew Baldwin, a kind and dedicated dentist who served the people of Wilmington with a smile. It would not take long for the two to be wed. Andrew had a thriving practice, but a small home. So when he and Emma were married, they had a larger two story home built on South Front Street. Dr. Baldwin would see his patients on the ground floor, while Mrs. Baldwin would keep the house upstairs private.

Emma Baldwin loved her home near the river. It was new and fancy, with the cachet of having a prominent doctor's shingle out front. She was deserving of respect, even more now. She had added to her family name, along with the status of her husband. He was a doctor, no mere laborer, a day to day worker. A dentist had skills. He had to study and pass license testing. He had to be good at what he did. She was very proud of her husband, but she was more proud of herself for being his wife.

Dr. Baldwin didn't have the same perceptions of himself, which quietly irked his wife. Andrew served anyone who needed treatment, and at the turn of the twentieth century, tooth care was still a skill practiced only on occasion for many people. When someone had a cavity, Andrew would do his best to help fill it. He benefited from new advances that had just occurred. He now had a power drill to clean the cavities, along with porcelain jackets for whole teeth, and best of all, a German scientist had invented a new pain reliever over in Europe. It had been called Procraine there, but the marketers who sold it in America gave it another name, Novocaine.

The change in dentistry meant that he could do more care, for more people, from all walks of life. While even the rich did have better hygiene, and better diets, everyone, rich or poor, had some tooth problems. Dr. Baldwin didn't turn anyone away.

To Emma, this was both a benefit, and a detriment.

She saw the well off come in to her home, "They have to come to you," she had insisted to her husband, to be treated. Dentistry was specialized. Dr. Baldwin couldn't cart a dental chair and tools around to the houses of the wealthy. It meant that their care, no matter how delicate, was a part of Emma's life. She was able to see into their mouths, through the words of her husband, who, after his day was over, would casually mention the treatments he did.

He would reveal who had good teeth, and who didn't take care of themselves. Other, more delicate diseases were not hidden from his close eye, and Dr. Baldwin knew all the secrets. He was a decent man, but also a decent and devoted husband. He never kept things from his wife.

Emma benefited from the juiciest of gossip in that her husband could easily give her a tooth by tooth description of the life of most people in Wilmington. She knew who was good at their health care. She knew who was not. Soon, she saw herself as an impeccable judge of character. She could tell just how "acceptable" a person was. An abscessed tooth, or a casual mention of lipstick on a collar, and the occasional "cousin" of a wealthy man coming in for needed care all gave her insight, along with the usual rough and ready dwellers of the wharf, who suffered from more cavities and loose tongues when the Novocaine took ahold of them.

What was the detriment was that the same poor people who came in, spilling their own secrets, or the wealthy asking to have their secrets kept, often didn't have money to pay. Or didn't want to have a trail of payments to the dentist showing up on their doorstep later on.

Emma Baldwin became a very proud judge of character, and very proud of her social stature with her successful dentist husband in their fancy new home. Right up until the time the bank came asking for missed payments on their loan.

Emma was incensed. This was *her* home. She had built it, no matter what it was used for. No one should be able to take it from her. An upturned nose and a judgy smirk told whoever was looking just what she thought of the bank. Her opinion of anyone who questioned what had happened to their house was just as well produced. No one wanted to be on the sharp end of a pointed nose and glaring stare of Emma Baldwin.

Perhaps it was Emma's tone, or more likely the clients of the well liked Dr. Baldwin came through with enough cash to cover the debts, but their house debt was paid, and the Baldwins resided in their beautiful home until the ends of their lives.

Emma Baldwin would live to a very ripe old age, passing away peacefully of natural causes. The grave was dug and the body was buried, but most now say the spirit didn't plant. Emma remained in her home.

Her home.

The house was sold, and new people moved in, not knowing they had a ghostly tenant. When they finally realized it, they didn't like how she paid her rent.

The new owners started discovering teeth in the house. At first, it just seemed like they were the unhappy remains of a dental practice that had to pull more than a few rotten incisors and molars. But they kept coming.

Emma was making her presence felt. Her ghost would leave teeth to people she didn't like. Occasionally, she would leave a dime, if she thought in her expert judgement that the person deserved her esteem.

One group of people she certainly did not want in her home were unmarried couples. She would not only leave them her rotten teeth, but also bang doors or push people on the stairs, *her* stairs, the narrow and slippery steps that were part of her time, but not safe for more modern dwellings.

Emma's ghost would be seen as one who wanted to keep not only her home, but also her place in society. She enjoyed being the judge of others. Even in her home as a ghost, she was the one privy to the most secret of secrets, and she thought she was the one to mete out her appraisal and punishment or reward. After all, she was here first.

It would take time, and lots of tenants, but Emma may have calmed down a little. She just wanted people to show her some respect. When a family moved into the haunted Baldwin house, *Emma's house*, the first thing they did was to talk directly to the spirit, wherever she was. They told her that they were moving in, but that they wanted Emma to know she was part of the house, and that they wanted to get along. It seems that all Emma wanted was someone to recognize her, her value, her place in the home she built.

On the upstairs window they found two dimes.

Maco Light

Maco

Charles Baldwin knew the story of Maco Light by heart. He has heard it so many times, he knows all the parts, from the sad beginnings, to the crash, the aftermath, and all the stories from then on of people seeing the light for decades afterward.

His name helped, he guessed. Joe Baldwin was the name of the poor conductor that lost his head in the wreck, and even though he was no relation to Charles, having the same surname gave him a small part of the attachment to the story.

He had heard the story for years. Decades. Everyone around Wilmington knew it by heart...

Joe Baldwin had moved back to Wilmington after fighting in the Civil War. He was a survivor of the last campaigns and battles, including Gettysburg. Joe was a fortunate person, however fortunate a person could be to go through that much death, and still survive. He was content, if not happy, to be a conductor for the Wilmington and Manchester Railroad. He slept in the caboose because it wasn't quite time to announce the last stop before Wilmington, at the little town of Maco.

When Joe awoke, he knew something was wrong immediately. There was no regular rocking, the rhythmic *clickclack* that every train car made as they traveled the line. The caboose was slowing, but the rest of the train was not. His car had come uncoupled from the train.

It would have been nothing more than worrisome to Joe that he would be stranded in the car on a dark, moonless night, and he would have to walk miles until he found any civilization. That would be difficult, but merely a trouble. It was not serious.

What was serious was that the caboose sat on darkened tracks in the middle of a dark night, and a high speed freight was the next train to be passing on the line. Joe had to find a way to signal it to slow down.

When the big freight train started to barrel down the track, Joe furiously waved his lantern in an attempt to warn the engineer. He knew it was a fruitless task, but he had to try. He saw the light of the freight train barreling toward him in the darkness. His little red lantern glowed so feebly by comparison. At the last moment, as the light shone in his face, he heard the train apply the brakes, squealing down from its horrendous onrushing pace, to no avail.

The train struck Joe and the caboose. The little car was turned to splinters. Joe's lantern was flung into the swamps of Maco. Joe's body was thrown a hundred feet into a grove of old, twisted trees. In the accident, his head was lopped off, decapitated.

The freight train barely was slowed by the caboose, and no one else was even hurt. By daylight, the search would commence for the mortal remains of poor Joe Baldwin, a man who stayed at his post to save lives, while he lost his after surviving so much death in the past. It would only take moments to find most of Joe, but his head would never be located.

About a year later, a couple waited at the small depot of Maco for the train and a trip into Wilmington. Down the tracks they saw a strange light bobbing toward them. It was near where the accident had happened. But as they watched, first mesmerized, they saw that the light had no source! No lantern made it, and no hand held a lantern, and no body held a hand! Now they were terrified, but unable to move. The strange scratchy ball of light wobbled its way up the tracks to the depot. They worried what would happen when it got to them. At the moment one began to speak, the light blinked out. For a heartbeat, they were able to relax and breathe a heavy sigh.

Then the light appeared on the other side of the depot, continuing its lopsided wander down the tracks until it vanished in the humid darkness.

It wouldn't take long for them to tell their strange story to friends in Wilmington. No one truly believed them, of course. Not until the next night, when the same bounding light appeared again along the tracks.

It wouldn't take long for the locals to realize that poor Joe Baldwin was back at work. He carried his signal lamp still, waving it up and down the track to warn any trains that his caboose was still on the tracks. Most figured he was trying to find a way to right a wrong where he saw himself to blame for causing the wreck, even though everyone knew it was something that he couldn't have helped.

Others had a more morbid thought. Maybe Joe was still out there, looking for his head. Until he was put back together, his spirit couldn't rest. But there was no way to find what was left of poor Joe Baldwin. His remains were interred in a grave in Wilmington, while his head was lost to the mire of Maco. So the light would walk the tracks for as long as they were there.

This would end up being true. The light, now known as Maco Light, would appear so regularly that people could easily predict its appearance. So common was the light that the trains that ran along the tracks had to use two signal lamps as markers for other trains. Engineers and conductors were thrown into panic by seeing the Maco Light along the tracks, thinking it might be another train they approached. The strange two light system was so unique that it was noticed by President Grover Cleveland. Even the president could not keep quiet as he asked about the lights and was given the otherworldly explanation.

For decades after, the Maco Light would appear to anyone with the patience to wait in the dark. Tourists in the 1950s who came to Carolina Beach would often stop in Maco, just to see the light. Kids would be at the ready, with crab nets in hand, in hopes of capturing the sparkling ether that flew across the tracks. Even soldiers from Fort Bragg once tried to surround the light, only to have it vanish inside the circle and appear just outside the ring of troops.

The light would appear most nights, especially around thunderstorms, when the air was thick, charged and spooky, to add to the ambience. Even when the trains stopped running, Joe Baldwin and the Maco Light kept up the appearances. The light would glow until 1977, when the tracks would finally be pulled up and the rail line disappeared into the pines and swamps. The only thing left were a few pilings from the old depot, hidden in the trees. Joe Baldwin walked the line no more.

Of course, Charles Baldwin knew all this was hogwash, poppycock, nonsense. There was no Joe Baldwin. He was just a figment of someone's imagination. The light was real, yes, but Joe Baldwin, no. That was just a story made up to get sympathy for an old soldier.

There wasn't even a train wreck in Maco in 1866. Charles would snort in derision at any idea of that. Maco wasn't even there in 1866. It wasn't anything but maybe a few small farms, with no name at all. It was named Maraco in the 1890s, and later shortened to Maco.

Charles Baldwin was certain of all these facts. He knew, without a doubt, that nothing like the legend said had ever happened.

He would stake his life on it.

If he had one.

Charles knew that the legend of Joe Baldwin wasn't true, because Charles Baldwin was the one who died in that train accident, ten years earlier, in 1856. He had been left with several cars, a few miles outside of Wilmington, while the train engine went ahead to get help for repairs on the cars. When the engine came back, late in the evening, it came in too fast. Charles had not hung a lamp on his cars to mark their location, and the fast moving train engine had plowed into his mail car, killing him, head and all, and injuring the mail agent, too.

Charles, the dead man, he would often point out, got the blame for not putting a lantern out.

He would die three days after the accident at the hospital in Wilmington. Charles Baldwin, head and all, was buried in the newly built Oakwood Cemetery, where he sits by his grave marker, an invisible ghost, ready and willing to tell his story to anyone who can hear him, which sadly is no one. Now that they pulled up the tracks, he has no more light to shine, either.

"It would be alright," he thought, "if they hadn't moved my grave."

When Oakdale was new, the graves got shifted, as more people were re-interred from small cemeteries. Charles Baldwin had his grave moved, too. They first took his headstone. But when they came back, they didn't know where his coffin was, so it was never moved. Charles Baldwin's body rests somewhere in an unmarked grave.

Joe Baldwin only lost his head. Charles Baldwin lost his whole body.

The Brunswick Inn

Southport

This story doesn't start in Southport. It may start in New York City, where a young man named Antonio Caseletta and several friends decided to head south to ply their trade in the warmer climates as musicians. It may even have started earlier than that, when Antonio's father, a skilled painter, immigrated from his home in Italy, taking his family, including seven year old Antonio, to America for a chance at a better life.

How does it end? Well, that's part of the story, isn't it?

Antonio was blessed with a similar artistic talent as his father, only in Antonio's case, it was with music. He played, among other instruments, the harp, a beautiful and often haunting instrument that added a silky depth to any band. New York City was full of places to play. It was also full of other musicians, and it was crowded, cold, and difficult to make a way in life. Antonio had the mixed blessing of being married, and a father of a newborn, at the young age of nineteen.

With an eye toward the open and warmer climes of the south, perhaps with hopes of finding a more Mediterranean climate like his homeland, Antonio, his wife and child, joined Pasquale Pascucci's band and took a steamship to Wilmington in hopes of finding work as musicians in greener pastures.

Wilmington turned out to be less welcoming to Antonio than he had hoped. While it was a large and functioning port city, with people from all around the world appearing out of ships that appeared out of the Atlantic, Antonio found that he and his company stood out as much as anyone would have who had as many mixed vowels, consonants, and syllables in his obviously foreign name.

Fortune fell upon the group, however, as the local ship captains were more used to different ports of call. They were accepting to the wonderfully varied people of each and every place they docked. A local skipper suggested the band to the Hotel Brunswick as a house band. They auditioned and were quickly contracted to play for the guests. Antonio was particularly noted as a talented and beautiful harpist who created a wonderful and melancholy sound on the instrument. The fine hotel and the small village had no problem with Antonio's heritage. He was an outstanding harpist, and a kind, fun person. He was also a devoted husband and father to his infant child.

So the band played and the people came. During the summer of 1882, the Hotel Brunswick would be filled with couples dancing the evening away to Pascucci's band and Antonio's harp playing. The young man would become a well liked part of the town. Any prejudice over Antonio and his name was washed away in the Cape Fear, as he quickly became known just as Tony.

The summer of 1882 would pass by fast, and come to and end too soon for Tony. He was invited with some other bandmates to go on a sailing trip one afternoon out into the Cape Fear River. The day went smoothly until it was time to come back to Southport. There was an issue with the sails, and the sailing craft foundered in the deep part of the river. With the sailboat tipping over and taking on water, the ballast in the hull shifted and it quickly capsized. The other members of the band and the captain were able to save themselves, but poor Tony drowned in the accident. He struck his head on the boat as it tipped, knocking him unconscious. He passed away on August 23, 1882, at the young age of only nineteen, leaving behind a grieving young widow and a child who would never know him.

The band, in mourning over their loss, but still having to play, left Tony's harp out with an empty seat to remember him that night. As they began to play their instruments, at first the tune felt a little empty without Tony's melodic harp. Then, something amazing happened.

The harp began playing all by itself, in tune with the band's music. The guests were amazed, as it happened right in front of them as they danced. They all realized what was happening. Tony had come back to play one more time.

Tony Caseletta would end up remaining at the Brunswick Inn even after death. His ghost has remained a permanent resident of the building even as it changed hands through changes in decades and centuries. His life as a father was cut too short, so he has been known to be rather devoted to any children that stay in the building that was once the Brunswick Inn. He would turn lights on during dark nights, close windows before a storm, or tuck children in with blankets.

He also is perpetually a nineteen year old, as well. He  has played plenty of tricks, which most of the residents just consider harmless pranks. He liked to go through the guests suitcases and grips, looking for delicate intimate wear that would have seemed foreign to him when he was a poor musician. He also admires jewelry, trinkets to some, but a gift he would have desired to give to his young wife. He often moved or left things out, just to surprise the guests.

Tony has remained at the Brunswick Inn as it has transferred back and forth from inn to private residence. His remains were placed in the old Smithville Burying Grounds in town, along with many other famous permanent residents to the old cemetery. But his spirit as always remained an active part of Southport.

Orton Pool Hall

Wilmington

"Willie… William… and Wil,"

The greatest pool player of all time, Willie Mosconi, once graced Wilmington's oldest pool hall with a game that was one for the legends. And in the same time, he may have befriended a rather strange and mysterious ghost that called the Orton Hotel home.

The only problem, one that Willie Mosconi may not have known, as he was just passing through the city, was that the Orton Hotel was long, long gone.

The Orton Hotel was built in 1888. The four story hotel was the finest, fanciest place to grace the waterfront, a true luxury stop for those coming or going from the bustling port city. In order to maintain the air of elegance, all the necessities of hotel life, the business end, such as the laundry, were hidden from the patrons' view by putting them in the basement.

They also hid, with a nod and a wink to the gentlemen who wished to partake, a pool room downstairs. It was a place for men to go for a quick round of pocket billiards. It was an escape from the society above ground. The men found it fortunate to have the pool tables down in the basement, and the pool hall itself would find relative good fortune decades later.

In 1949, the Orton would catch fire and burn. Everything above ground would turn to ash and dust, crumbling away to nothing. All that would be left was underground in the basement, which included the laundry, the barber shop, and the pool hall.

Fortunately for those staying at the hotel, the fire spread slowly enough that all the registered guests were alerted and rescued from the burning hotel. What no one would know until much later, as they searched through the wrecked building, was that they would find the remains of one more man.

Apparently a man had come to Wilmington at the last minute to be with his older brother, who was sick and on his deathbed in a nearby hospital. With no time nor the inclination to find a room, he simply snuck into the Orton and stayed in an unoccupied room. Sadly for him, the man named William "Bill" Stevens preceded his ill brother in death.

Once the debris of the hotel was cleared, the Orton was born anew when the Orton Pool Room opened soon after. It was a low ceiling dark hall, with the tables lit like islands in a gloomy shadow ocean. It had the wonderful aura that any true pool hall needed for concentrated play.

Or for a ghost to haunt.

In 1956, Willie Mosconi would go on tour to play pool in exhibition matches across the country. He had been playing against the best players in the US since he was only six, and now at forty years old was considered the greatest to ever play the game. Pool players flocked to meet the man and see him play. Willie was used to the attention and liked it. He especially took a liking to one man, a handsome blond gentleman who seemed interested in the game, but also distracted. The man's name was Bill. Willie had seen him talking to a woman earlier. Willie Mosconi liked having another William around, in addition to being in Wilmington.

The Orton Pool Hall was already a landmark at the time. It had been in operation in the 1800s, a rare feat to have it still exist, and be open. Willie knew this was a place to be, and it was going to be a special night. He felt it.

Willie talked amiably with the other guests. He was happy to be out, talking with the others about his new wife and recent marriage. He was the spokesman for the game. He looked good and comfortable at the tables. With a nod to some of the onlookers, including the blond Bill, he commenced to play.

And what a game they saw! Never in the history of pool had there ever been someone play with such finesse and touch. Wille played straight pool, a difficult game, especially on the standard smaller tables tucked into the cramped basement of the Orton. Pool players at their best are so skilled that they will place the cue ball in the right place for the next shot as they shoot the one before. Wille seemed to be in an unparalleled zone. He would strike the cue with such a deft touch that the billiard balls would roll right to the pockets, then stop, seemingly to freeze in a moment as if they would not fall, then finally, with a gasp from the crowd, tumble into the soft pockets with a muffled thump or click.

On that night, Willie Mosconi would shoot a record number of 365 consecutive balls without a miss, a documented fact observed by all who witnessed the event. To this day, the only person to break that record in a competition would be Willie Mosconi himself.

As the shots went on, longer and longer, the crowd remained silent, as if a sound might break the magic. Willie didn't fear the sound, but he didn't mind the attention as his number went higher. At 365, he paused to note that it was one for every day of the year. Looking up at the crowd, he noticed his fellow William, the blond man, was not there.

"Hey, where did William go?" Most all of the crowd didn't know who he referred to. A young woman spoke up.

"He said he had to go up to the fourth floor. He had some business to do for his brother."

Willie just shook off the comment with a smile. It had been a long evening, and he couldn't expect everyone to stick around. The guy was looking out for family, Willie thought. Nothing wrong with that.

But the rest of the room got a slight chill after the woman spoke. Instead of silence, there were a few murmurs.

"There's no fourth floor. This is a one story building."

No one else had seen this man. No one knew who Willie was talking about.

Again, with the same ease and comfort, Willie Mosconi lined up his shot. He drew his cue back, struck the white ball true, which kissed the billiard ball with the distinctive *click* that all pool players know so well. The ball rolled toward the pocket, and just like many times before, came to a rest just on the edge.

But this time, the ball stopped. It didn't fall.

Legend says that Willie and William, the ghost from the Orton Hotel fire, worked together to put on a show for the guests of the Orton Pool Hall. When the billiard balls came close, Bill's invisible ghostly fingers would give the ball a nudge, letting it fall into the pocket. Willie didn't mind. It was fun. It was a show. It was just a couple of Williams looking out for each other on a dark night in a pool hall.

The Hanging Tree

Wilmington

Terry Spruill had several things going for him. He was rather good looking. His parents were rather wealthy. He was rather well liked by the other students in his high school in Wilmington.

He was also rather impetuous and rather impulsive, with a sense of humor that was unencumbered by the filters that other people had that whispered to them, "Maybe we shouldn't do this."

So it was a good thing he had those other things going for him. Because if he didn't, he would have been kind of a moron.

"Hey," he poked at a couple of his friends in school one day, "Let's take the new guy out to Airlie Road and show him the Hanging Tree!"

The "new guy" was David Cho, who was not a "new guy" by any stretch. He had come to their school that year, a fifteen year old sophomore, and now was a pitcher on the baseball team along with Terry and his friends. Everyone liked David. Terry just thought it would be a good way to show he was part of the team by taunting him with a spooky ghost story. This was only the latest time that Terry's filter was not working well.

But people went along with Terry. He was also rather charming, in a harmless, kind of stupid way, which made things fun for everyone else. He was usually the one to get into trouble with whatever they did, so it worked out all around. At least, that was the way teenage boys saw it.

"Aw, man," commented one of the boys, Case Charity, "I hate that story. It's just wrong. And David didn't do nothing to us. He's an okay kid." Case, at seventeen and a year older than most of the others, had grown out of the usual pranks of high school life. He counted the months until he could get out of high school and go to college to play ball.

"No, listen," argued Terry with a devious smile on his face, "c'mon, we need to let him into the group." Terry somehow figured that befriending a fellow student whom he already knew for six months involved dark nights and death somehow. "We just tell him the story, then take him out there. We get one of you to go rub the roof of the car with a tree branch or something, see if we can freak him out. We'll invite some girls," Terry always wanted to invite the girls, who rarely ever came when he asked, "and we can go back to my place and party." Again, his idea of party was probably playing video games and failing to steal his father's liquor, but the other guys knew it would be entertaining. Terry was always entertaining.

The story of which Terry spoke was an old urban legend. Down toward the end of Airlie Road, near the big Aerlie Gardens with its mile of trees lining the waterfront, was an old oak that overhung the road. The old legends said it was a place for hanging, or punishment, meted out by sea captains or evil landowners. The horrors of the past had morphed into more mundane but still creepy legends. If a person drove down the road at night, they could see the big branch stretched out high across the road. After they pass, if they look back in the mirror, or over their shoulder, a ghostly silhouette will form in the night. A figure will be seen hanging from a rope off the tree branch, a victim of punishment meted out fair or foul, from a time long past. If you try to back up to see the ghostly appearance, it vanishes into the night.

"Man, that story isn't scary, and it's not funny, either," Case replied to Terry's plan. "Don't go messing with David, doin' something stupid. The last thing we need to do is get him in trouble." As good a baseball player as Case was, he knew that David was as great a pitcher. They didn't need the kid wrapped up in one of Terry's pranks.

"We won't mess with him," Terry insisted. "We'll just take him with us, let him get a little scared. Everyone does it." He fairly whined the last bit.

"Man, you think that is funny?" Case shook his head. "I don't mind us hanging out, but I'm not doing anything to the kid."

Terry tried to brush off the Case's brush off. He knew he could get a few of his teammates to go along if he promised food and a party. "Okay, we'll get someone else to go with us. Don't worry, we won't hurt David," Terry tried to act like Case was the one who was immature, but Case just shook his head and went off to class early. He had his AP chemistry to worry about, not some silly hazing prank.

That Saturday night, Terry borrowed his father's big Audi so that he could fit more people in the car. David, the youngest and smallest, sat in the middle of the back. "I'm tellin' ya, Cho, you are gonna *love* this." Terry was beaming with pride at showing off the urban legend to his teammate. He had told David the basic idea of the story. Now it was dark and cool, with a soft quarter moon cutting through the cloudy night sky. Terry had found some of his dad's music to fit the mood, playing *Don't Fear The Reaper* by Blue Öyster Cult. He thought that would be cool.

"So, listen, man, here's the story. If you drive down Airlie Road at night, at a night like this..." he decided to try to sound scary, "you will see the branch hanging over the road. But when you pass and look back, you'll see a body hanging from the tree. And if you try to turn around, it vanishes.

"But here's the really cool thing," Terry went on, promising more than the legend usually allowed. "If you park under the tree at night, turn of the engine and put the keys on the roof, then when you wait in the dark... you'll start to hear the body swaying above you. Then you hear his feet rubbing on the roof of the car!"

Terry and his pals relished the slight bit of fear they got from David. Who wouldn't be a little scared? The thought of a dead man's feet, the body blown by the wind, slowly swaying just above your head. And you had to reach back up on the roof to get your keys to start the car and get out of there!

But David wasn't going to show how scared he was. He was part of the team. Many of them were his friends, and as dumb as Terry seemed, he also seemed a little harmless. He wasn't drinking, or driving fast, anything like that. He just wanted to tell a story, maybe scare David a little. It was part of being part of the team, so David went along with it.

They drove down the road in the dark of the evening. No other cars were out at the time, and the road was empty. As they got nearer, they could all see the branch overhanging the road. David actually saw less of it, being in the back middle, and to his delight, he felt the car get a little colder and quieter as the other boys became a little less brave.

Terry was too tied up in his own gleeful plans to notice. He pulled over right under the tree. No ghostly body of a hanged man showed up, no telltale shadows in the mirror. David almost expected someone to just come up and bang on the window, and he said so.

"No, be quiet, just wait," insisted Terry. He turned the engine off, along with the headlights. The dash went dark.

Then Terry cursed, turned on the electrics, rolled the window down, and turned the car off again. He was afraid his forgetting he had power windows might have ruined the magic. With a soft *chlink*, he sat the keys on the roof, careful not to scratch his father's car.

"Okay, now… wait…" he said in a whisper.

Nothing happened for a little while. None of the boys were willing to be the one to break the silence first, though. David didn't know what was going to happen, and Terry waited with anticipation at what would.

Finally, after an agonizing minute in the dark had passed, they all heard a soft sound. Something brushed against the roof of the car.

David looked at the others, waiting for a smile or a laugh, but he didn't get one. They looked a little scared, too.

Then another sound, longer this time, like a broom sweeping across the roof. Then back the other way.

"There he is!" insisted Terry in a sotto voce whisper meant to hide him from the ghost on the roof but be heard in the car. "That's him, on the roof!"

David noticed one of his teammates shrink a little from the inside of the car. The strange swooping sounds happened a few more times.

Then there was a soft scrape.

"Dude," asked one of the other boys, "what was that?"

Terry didn't like that sound. That wasn't the sound he was supposed to hear. Then it happened again. Louder.

There was a keening scrape, like the dead body's toenails were now digging across the expensive German paint job. "H…" at first Terry wanted to yell out, get the scratching to stop, but it would mean giving away the secret. Then the scratching happened again, more, and more.

"Let's go, Terry," asked another boy. "This is a little too weird for me. It's not what's supposed…" *skreeeeeee* "to happen." The last two words ended up more high pitched than he would have liked.

Terry agreed wordlessly, and reached up to get the keys as fast as he could.

They weren't there.

He felt the breath leave him, and he got cold and sweaty at the same time. His hand pounded on the roof, feeling for the keys. "C'mon, man," his friends insisted.

"I can't find the keys!"

"Get out and look for them! They probably fell on the ground!"

Terry was not going to get out of the car, not now. For a moment, he looked back, thinking…

"Oh no," said David, "I'm okay with a little messing with the new guy, but I'm not getting out of this car and have you leave me on the street!" He still thought this was some strange prank.

Terry stuck his hand out one more time. This time, he felt the keys on the roof, right where he left them. He started the car and slammed it into Drive, spinning the tires for a heartbeat while the big Audi found grip on the gravel and the traction control kicked in. They spun out of the dirt onto the dark road and drove quickly toward the turn to Wrightsville Beach. Terry hastened a glance in his side mirror. There in the dark, lit by his taillights, was just the faint shadow of the tree branch, empty.

They all got back to Terry's house, a little scared, but now able to laugh about it. "David, you took it better'n I did," one player said.

"Man, that was a little spooky," said another. "That wasn't funny."

When they pulled up to the drive, the kids could barely wait to get out. They spilled from the back seat and ran toward the lights of the front porch and the safety of doors they could close behind them. Terry chased after his friends.

The rest of the team was already out back. The night turned cool, and they had a fire in a large metal pit going. Some of the guys ate pizza while they stood around with a few of their girlfriends who were willing to show up at Terry's place.

Terry saw Case there already. He looked at Case, then looked down. Terry wasn't entirely proud of what he did, but he knew he couldn't admit it. He then looked up and smiled a little. He walked over and said, "You shoulda been there, man. We had him going for a minute."

Case shook his head. "You think that stuff is funny? You shouldn't be teasing the guy."

Just at that moment, Terry saw another player come out of the darkness. He walked over and grabbed the boy's arm. "What were you doing, man?" Terry hissed. "You were just supposed to rub a branch on the roof for a minute."

"What are you talking about?"the boy answered. "I tried to tell you…"

"You were scratching up the car. You better hope you didn't actually put a scratch on it. My dad will kill me."

"First of all, your dad won't kill you. He's never done anything to you," the boy insisted. "And I tried to tell you. I never went out there. Heck, I figured this was another of your pranks and you were trying to leave me in the dark, like you would do to Cho over there."

"What do you mean, you didn't go?" Terry got cold, his eyes big in the dark night.

At that moment, Terry heard his father call him.

"Terry, what did you do to the car?!"

Mr. Spruill led Terry out to the front drive, followed by most of the baseball team and several girls who seemed a little delighted to see Terry in trouble for once. "What do you mean, Dad?" Terry asked innocently.

Wordless, Mr. Spruill walked over to his car, motioning Terry to come with him. Terry was looking at the fenders and tires to see if he had a flat, or if it was dirty or dented.

Then his father pointed to the roof.

There, on the sparkling gray metallic paint, scratched across the roof, were these words…

DO YOU THINK THIS IS FUNNY?

Money Island

Wilmington

Pirates of the 1600s must have seen the coast of North Carolina as a pristine barren emptiness of waving salt grasses and undulating yellow sand dunes. The thin barrier islands, littered with shells from a thousand years before, but not disfigured yet by a single footprint of Man, offered shelter from the hunters of the Royal Navy, as well as a stalking blind for the treacherous buccaneers to hunt the ships that passed by on their way north or south, laden with riches in gold, silk and linen, or anything fine that pirates might plunder.

It would have been a peaceful scene that one pirate, Captain William Kidd, would have seen as he passed the islands off of the Cape Fear river, where Wilmington would be founded some forty one years later. In 1699, only a few settlers found any purchase on the land. None would be on the empty marsh near the future Wrightsville Beach and Intracoastal Waterway. At that time, the land and water would be blissfully calm and empty.

That was the way Captain Kidd wanted it. He found an empty abyss to bury his treasure. Kidd was returning from his trip to the Caribbean where he had sailed as a privateer captain. Unfortunately for him, he had moved from chartered privateer to being labeled a pirate, for multiple reasons, including the murder of one of his own crewmen. His plan was to bury his treasure along the coast, then return empty handed to New York, where he would plead his case to hopefully friendly government agents. If not, the treasure would serve to hopefully bribe his way to freedom.

Instead, he was taken in chains to London, where he was found guilty of murder and piracy. He was ultimately hanged until dead, though it took two attempts on the condemned captain. The first rope snapped when he fell, and had to be hanged twice, the second time at the opposition of the crowd, who saw the breaking rope as a sign he should go free. The pleas fell to deaf ears. Kidd was again hanged, this time until he was dead. Then his body was tied and strung over the Thames River for two years to rot in a grotesque reminder of what happens to those who go against King and Crown. Pirates Beware.

He should have stayed in North Carolina.

Kidd had buried his treasure on a small interior island. He marked the spots of two iron chests, laden with gold, by planting two sapling trees over each. In order to protect the plunder, he left a trusted sailor, John Redfield, to guard the treasure, with the mistaken promise that Kidd would come back. When Kidd finally met his end and the end of a rope,

Redfield, worried about threats to his own life by pirates looking for the treasure, snuck away to Charleston where he lived a more comfortable life off of his take of the booty. He would ultimately tell his story to his children and grandchildren, who would then go looking for the lost treasure. An old broken chest was once found, along with a few gold coins, but the bulk of the prized hoard was never located.

Except possibly by one person.

Dr. George Worth returned to his home of Wilmington for the first time in five years. He served as the head of a missionary group in China, and always came back home with stories and gifts from the exotic Far East.

And every five years, he came back home with a new discovery that he would share with the children of his family and friends. He would open a wrapped package, marked with strange symbols or unusual peregrine stamps, with a conspiratorial grin, saying he found it deep within a dusty old shop in the back alleys of a market square. It could be an ornate box, or a dusty bottle, or an old painting faded with age. Within it he would pull out a map, its edges burned and yellow, with a flourishing script of black ink written in Old English. On it would be a map of the Wilmington coast, along with a close up of what was now known as Money Island. This was, he would decree, the real and true map of Captain William Kidd, showing the only path to find his hidden treasure.

Of course, the directions supplied as well a warning. The treasure was protected, cursed, and could only be found on certain nights, when the lights and tides were just right. How fortunate, he would point out, that the date coming up fell on one of those times, with a bright full moon to light their way.

While the little ones squealed and wiggled at the prospect of digging for pirate gold, the older kids, teenagers mostly, had more devious smirks on their faces that they failed to entirely hide. They had heard this story before, and now they were in on the hunt.

The day that they were scheduled to go over to Money Island, Dr. Worth would gather a sack of trinkets, costume jewelry, and a few near worthless coins from foreign lands, and take a boat to the island to salt the sand with "treasure" for the little ones to find. He purposely made sure to plant the booty within easy reach, only a few inches deep in the sand, or just under the reeds of the scrub brush that grew plentifully on the south part of the island.

No one came with him during the day to do this. It was his and his alone to fulfill this task. So no one noticed how he purposefully avoided the northern part of the island, a tall rise of sugar loaf sand surrounded by a tangled mess of sharp seagrass.

Later that night, the first boats would row over to Money Island. These would be filled with the teenage boys and girls who had once been part of the treasure expedition in years past when Dr. Worth would arrive with his map. Over the past twenty years, he must have found four or five of them, they joked.

Their job was to hide in the grass, or climb the trees in the darkness. When the little kids got close, they would softly hiss or whistle, making ghostly sounds as the promise of ghosts just off in the dark, ready to pounce if they stray too far off the path to the gold.

Then, with the last strands of light appearing over the western horizon, more boats would come, loaded with adults and children. They would come over with adults and children. The kids were all bearing flashlights while the adults carried gas lanterns, their lights hissing out a white glow from the mantles. The children would jump off the boats and storm the shore with shovels clanking as they hit the sand. The buckets they carried made a more hollow noise, and the whole milieu became a strange mix of exotic percussion and high pitched song of kids squealing with terrified delight.

As soon as the children made it to the edge of the shore, they would stop as they realized they had no idea where to look. Dr. Worth had the map, where was he? They were ready to charge into the unknown, fight the dreaded pirate ghosts and vanquish them to take their gold and escape as the heroes.

Only when all the kids were ashore would Dr. Worth step out of the tall grass, dressed in his finest safari hat, or whatever he found to be the most striking for the children. He would flourish the map and read slowly from it, directing the kids to their first steps. The roundabout path would lead them around the small island, through the rolling hammocks, in and out of the stand of trees that seemed like an impenetrable forest to the little ones. All the while, dark shadows would move in the corner of their eyes. The ghosts were on the prowl, and ready to fight for their cursed gold and jewels. The treasure belonged to Captain Kidd, and his loyal crew was trusted to protect the ill gotten booty from any and all hands, big or small. In the distance, and sometimes closer than they liked, a ghost would moan a haunting call, sending the children into fits as they closed ranks for protection.

But Dr. Worth always kept them safe. He told them that as long as he had the map, and a lucky charm that he flashed, an old worn coin that glinted dully in the yellow moonlight as he flicked it deftly into his palm, the pirate ghosts couldn't harm them. When asked what the coin was, he just said it was an old pirate coin from long ago.

And what he said was true. The map led them on a path to the treasure, buried only inches beneath the surface, under or near the many trees that grew along the south end of Money Island. The kids went after their prizes with zeal. They dug and grabbed, sifting the sand for pearls on strands, rings with gems that sparkled like diamonds in the moonlight, and in the moonlight who could even tell that they were nothing but paste jewels. Rare coins from far away lands littered the sand. With their age and the strange writings on them, they must be worth a fortune, the kids thought. Mysterious Asian writings were etched on the coins, and the kids could only guess at what the words might read. How much money did they have, they wondered? Hundreds? Thousands? Millions, maybe? Dr. Worth didn't let them know that it was just extra change he brought back from China that was worth only a few dollars, along with some English and Spanish coins thrown in from his exchanges as he traveled across the Atlantic. To the children, the money was priceless, worth so much more than the penny candies they could buy with American change.

It took only minutes to dig all the treasure and recover the long lost loot of Captain William Kidd. He had no use for it, being stretched on a rope so long ago. The children would be able to tell stories and trade for prizes for the next year with envious neighbors and friends from school lessons. The older kids would filter out of the island once the little ones had made it to their boats, with their own stories of clandestine hiding places and terrifying calls in the night. The few scratches and bites were well worth the fun.

Dr. Worth of course was more pleased than anyone. He had put another successful treasure hunt under his belt. His family and his friends' families, the wealthy Sprunts that helped support him in his missionary service, who owned the island, all were thrilled with the night and the fun. They could all pile into the boats and head back to land, and light, the safety of home, to have treats and count the booty that the kids found, if the boys and girls even made it back to shore. Some were already falling asleep from the shift from the harrowing thrill of ghost chases to the rolling rhythm of the boats as they made their way back to their landings to the west.

But Dr. Worth would always remain behind, just a little longer than the others. He would say, only to the adults, that he wanted to make sure that all the treasure was found. But then he would tromp off to the northern section of the island, where no footprints had dared to tread in following the mysterious pirate map. Dr. Worth needed no pirate map to find his way, even on a darkened night with only moonlight to guide him.

The sand sparkled with a magical indulgence as if to lead Dr. Worth in his direction. He knew where he was going.

He walked with intention. He was a man who had done this walk before. Though in all his days as a missionary, treating the sick and injured, he had never dealt with this type of case anywhere else. He pushed his way through a tall and almost impenetrable thicket of seagrass. Going slowly to make sure he didn't get scratched by the sharp blades coated with salt rime, he kept his eyes peeled for the telltale signs of what, or who, he was looking for.

At the top of the low loaf, the sand laid bare. The trees surrounded the hill on all sides, which blocked all view from the water and marsh. As Dr. Worth made his way to the top of the hill, a soft blue light appeared in the treeline. It moved with impunity, not worried about the razor grass as it flowed through the thick brush. Dr. Worth watched, as he always did when he came to the hill every five years, mesmerized by the appearance. It took time, but the blue light formed the vague shape of a person. It always looked like the ghost had to work very hard just to piece himself together, just for this moment. The blue figure wavered from this existence into the netherworld from where he came, fighting to gain any measure of meaningful corporeal being. He finally solidified just enough to create the form of a sailor, a pirate or privateer from a time long ago.

Dr. Worth didn't know if this was Redfield or one of the other crew that had remained loyal to Captain Kidd upon his return to be judged. He just knew that this ghost had long guarded the treasure in the only way he could, by keeping it hidden from anyone but a chosen few who had learned the secret long ago. Dr. Worth was the only one left, and he helped protect Kidd's treasure, while keeping the lore of the pirates alive as well.

Dr. Worth pulled out a small bottle of rum, always something good, from his travels, and placed it on the sand in the middle of the hill. Then he pulled out his talisman, the dull coin he would flip to keep the "ghosts" at bay as the kids hunted. It was a real, true coin, an old French Louis d'or, a gold coin, and a prize for any English sailor looking to take from the enemy French. Dr. Worth flipped the coin down, and with a clink, it struck the bottle and landed in the sand.

The ghost mouthed a wordless gesture of thanks. The coin and bottle sank into the sand as the ghost almost breathed a sigh. It could now relax and disappear again, its job placated for another five years.

Dr. Worth turned and walked away quickly to his boat, with the same relaxed sigh.

The Price-Gause House

Wilmington

We all hide some of our secrets in little cabinets and closets throughout our homes. The mess we try to hide from the rest of the world gets shoved aside as we push harder and harder against that door to make it close.

Sometimes that door just won't shut. Or, even worse, it opens on its own.

That may be what has been happening at the Price-Gause house on the east side of Wilmington. The fancy Italianate home was built in 1860 by Dr. William Price to serve as his home and office. As Wilmington grew in importance at the time, land became more valuable, so Dr. Price was fortunate to find an open plot that was also big enough for his fancy edifice as well as still close to the river and the businesses along the banks of the Cape Fear.

If he had known the history of the land, he may have chosen another spot.

Soon after it was built, Dr. Price's house started having some strange ghostly events. Servants noticed that items were being moved in the kitchen overnight when no one was there. Strange sounds, the soft distant clinking of chains, were heard. Doors opened and closed on their own. On any old house, that would have been seen as simply the home no longer being level or square. But the new home of Dr. Price was well built, the best that his money could buy. There was definitely something strange going on in the house.

The house would pass through history with new residents and owners. By the time Captain Thomas Gause bought the house, the events had been passed down into expectations and legends. The premise that the house was haunted had moved from fear and speculation into acceptance of fact.

Shadowy figures moved in the house, just out of direct view, but the residents knew they were there. They just knew. People walking by would see a mysterious figure move a curtain and fade into the caliginous gloom of an unused room. The cold spots became part of the home, "it's just part of the charm!" of owning a haunted house. Far from being terrified, the haunting was embraced.

Even one of the ghosts, an old man, well dressed, obviously charming, was given the nickname George, though no one really knows who he is. His sobriquet unfairly invokes a simpleton, the name of a less than human pet almost. The ghost becomes both normalized and marginalized by giving him a name he neither was born with nor deserved.

But it makes the story so much nicer.

If only they knew the real truth, which is not in the house, but underneath. And before, as in the times long before the house was built.

There is a reason the land was clear and available, but Dr. Price would not know the full extent of that reason. Or he may have just waved it off, like the descendants did with the later ghosts of the house. Long before the Price-Gause house was built, the land it sat on was on the periphery of Wilmington. It was an edge, a corner, both feared and revered, for it was originally known as Gallows Hill.

In the late 1700s and well into the 1800s, this was one of the spots where convicted criminals were brought to meet their grisly end at the hangman's noose. Hanging at the time was more than a punishment, it was also a warning that if you committed a crime, you would get what the city said you deserved. A murderer would be led out from the jail in chains all the way to the gallows, a few rote words might be said, maybe to help his soul, more likely to mask the souls of those that watched, then a sack would be put over the killer's head, along with a rope. Hopefully, if the criminal had any money, or if the hangman had any compassion, the knot would be put to the side. The handle to the gallows would be thrown, and the convicted would fall, fall, fall…

Until the rope jerked and snapped his neck, making him dead, dead, dead…

Unless that knot was placed at the back of his head. Then the guilty would dance, dance, dance…

And the gathered crowds would cheer, cheer, cheer…

For some hangings, there would be over two thousand people in attendance, there to watch the worst among them fall. In a city of only 12,000 souls, that's a lot of people in one place. The number got bigger if you counted the dead over the years.

Again, if the convicted had money, or they had a family or friend to claim the body, they might be buried in a grave somewhere. If not, if they were paupers, indigent, the body wouldn't go very far. They were often buried in an unmarked shallow grave nearby.

Most of the people hanged at Gallow's Hill would be forgotten to time within days or weeks. Few, if any, would be reported in the newspapers of the time. But one of the many who died was James Pekham. He became famous for a moment when he was convicted of stealing a wealthy woman's purse. He continually maintained his innocence, even as he was marched up the gallows for his last moments. There, standing high above the crowd so he could fall far and they could see well, he spied not only the purse, but the man who had actually stolen it. He cried out that he saw the real culprit, a greedy and horrendous man who gleamed as he thought he would watch the last act of getting away with the crime. The onlookers seized the man, and a search was made for the purse, but nothing was found. Even with this doubt in everyone's mind, James Pekham was hanged within moments.

It has been speculated that his ghost is the strange shadowy figure seen wandering the halls and peering out windows. But he isn't alone.

The legends of the kindly George are possibly flights of fancy, created for tourists to delightfully shake and chill at the story, but not really be afraid. Who can be afraid of a ghost named George? What is real is the opposite of fancy. It's dirty and rather gruesome. In the yard surrounding the Price-Gause house are the bones and remains of those who were hanged and had nowhere left to go but in the ground.

People who lived in the house over the decades would find bits of bones, teeth, skulls, all the detritus of the dead and unwanted criminals, the convicted, even those that may have been innocent but had no chance to survive for another day. They lay equally in the ground, but never fully at rest.

Even today people say they feel the loss of life when they walk by the land that the house sits on. The bodies were planted in a potter's field which became an orchard for only bones to grow out of the tainted land. When the house was built decades later, the relative rest that the spirits had in poor soil became unrest. While the land seemed empty, it at least didn't have a house sitting on top of unmarked graves. When Dr. Price built his home, the spirits became restless, coming back up as best as they could, to stir the world of the living. The land often invokes a feeling of dread or nausea from those who have visited the side of the yard, one of the few places where the land is still open and uncovered by the house. A dreadful pressure, possibly the feeling of being buried or trapped, is often felt by visitors, who then have the strong urge to get away.

From the outside, to those who don't get close to experience the haunting firsthand, the Price-Gause House looks like one of the many fancy houses that have survived the eras and moved into the peaceful bliss of historical homes throughout Wilmington. But just like the messes hidden in our own closets, a closer look will always supply a darker, more complex side.

The Hunt For Theodosia

Bald Head Island

March 29, 1939

"No one's gonna believe me!"
"I'll believe you!"
"That's because you were there!"
This breathless and terse exchange took place between Bill Kirkwood and his girlfriend as they sat in the darkness of a boat, panting, covered in sweat and sand, from a terrifying nighttime sprint up the shore toward the small downtown of Bald Head Island.

"No one's gonna believe any of us," insisted a tall blond who manned the wheel of the small boat as it *putt-putted* its way from the docks, toward the safer shores of quiet Southport.

"And we're not gonna tell *anybody*!" added the young woman next to the blond.

The rest of the group looked at her, incredulous. They all had a story to tell; a mad, crazy story of terror. Ghosts, pirates, chases, screaming…

Maybe they shouldn't tell anyone, they all thought in their collective heads.

Oddly enough, only Bill Kirkwood would end up keeping the secret. Everyone else in his group of six told someone within the next day. So it was a surprise to only him when a reporter showed up at his door late the next morning. "Mr. Kirkwood? I'm Benjamin Harper, a writer for the State Port Pilot. I'd like to ask you about your adventure last night."

Bill was taken aback by the question. Even though the man seemed calm and polite, he thought that the group would keep their story a secret, at least for a few weeks. He barely got to sleep on it in the hopes it would turn out to be a bad dream.

"How did you hear about that?" Bill stammered, then quickly added, "I mean, *what* adventure?" Way to cover your tracks, Bill, he thought to himself.

"I think you should tell me what happened," said Harper, quietly, with the kind tone of a father who already knew what happened.

"I don't want this to get all over the island," said Bill. He waved his hand toward the other houses in his neighborhood.

"It's already there," answered Harper, "This just gives you and me a chance to tell the story correctly. Are you worried people won't believe you? I can guarantee you some people will believe your story.

"I'll believe you," Harper added, as a promise more than a prompt.

"Okay, well… Come around to the back. I'll tell you on the porch. You want a cup of coffee? I am going to need a cup of coffee." he was tired from the long night, and it was still too early for anything else.

Bill and Benjamin sat on the back porch of Bill's house, a clapboard home that had turned gray from years of wind and storms on the coast. "Are you sure you won't just laugh at me?" Bill asked.

"Look," again Benjamin took a comforting tone. He had done this before, Bill could tell. "I won't publish anything you don't want me to, alright? If I write it up and you don't want it told, I won't tell it. I have to live here, too, you know."

"Okay," sighed Bill, "here goes…"

Bill, his girlfriend, and two other couples had gone over to Smith Island that evening. The island had been bought about twenty years earlier, with grandiose plans for a boardwalk, hotel, and a casino, but not much had come of it. The island, a mishmash of three smaller islands, was largely uninhabited, except seasonally by hunters and fishermen. Old Baldy stood near the docks, and the skeleton of the taller Cape Fear Lighthouse towered black and empty, having been turned off years ago. Smith Island, and the ocean facing Bald Head Island that was part of it, was a wonderful place to wander and get lost for a day or evening.

The three couples had already explored the old lighthouse keeper's quarters, and the abandoned Coast Guard station, where all the windows were broken out and the rooms filled with sand from numerous storms that blew in off the Atlantic Ocean.

The day had turned into a glorious evening. On Bald Head, the sun would stretch over the southern beach, only to dip toward Oak Island toward the west, creating a glowing sunset across the glistening Atlantic. They were just sitting on the beach, snuggling up as the air got cool in late March, when they began to hear some strange noises come from the treeline. Thinking at first maybe some other lovers had come to the beach, Bill made a few coughing noises, as if to tell the hidden romantics to move on to more secluded land.

But the sounds became more pronounced.

"What is that, an animal?" asked his girlfriend Louise, a beautiful dark haired woman. Her short black hair framed a round face, with an upturned nose that looked cute to Bill, while her brown eyes were strikingly intelligent. She held a constant look of cleverness, while at the same time able to melt most men down with her soft brown eyes.

Bill knew that even on an island, animals could find their way down from the north, through the marshes, all the way to the soft bald headlands that gave the place its name.

"That's no animal," Bill said. They all could tell they heard voices, even distinct words, but they were unintelligible to them. They all stood up, looking to the woods.

Suddenly, with a near intractable terror, three figures burst from the treeline. The figures came at the group, with no sense of fear of being outnumbered. Bill and his friends were momentarily rooted to the sand, unaware of just how to respond. They all just stared, open mouthed, aghast.

The three figures glowed yellow and white in the dusky light. They barely touched the sand hills as they made their way at great pace toward Bill group. Each of the three were dressed in an antiquated garb, moldy and disheveled. They wore pantaloons over thin bare legs, with ripped shirts flowing over emaciated chests. In their arms they each brandished what appeared to be a ragged cutlass, the preferred weapon of choice of pirates for doing their bloodthirsty business on the confined decks of ships. But even the gleaming otherworldly weapons were not what terrified Bill and his friends into a near stupor.

While the horrifying ghostly pirates came charging at them, weapons drawn, cursing in some muffled and illiterate language, none of the three had their heads.

The six members of the party found their collective footing and took off in different directions. Two headed toward the old light house keepers quarters, while four raced west to the downtown, and the location of their boat. Within steps, they reached and pulled for each other, one way or another, they all desperately wanted to get away from these strange wraiths.

Bill bolted first. His girl, Louise, had gone toward the old lighthouse, and he reversed course to join her. The rest followed. They ran down the beach in terror as the strange ghost pirates chased after them. At a cut in the dunes, the six of them quickly turned inland toward any sense of protection. The trees and hills beckoned. It took minutes that seemed like an hour, but they found their way to the old keeper's house, where they huddled next to the door.

"What are those things?" Louise asked.

"They look like ghosts," another said. It was as obvious as it seemed. Glowing, strange figures from the past, angry, terrifying, and missing heads but still able to run and pursue their victims, they had to be. But it still helped them to have someone say it out loud. Just because it was so unbelievable.

"Why do they want us?" shrieked one of the other girls. "What did we do? What were they yelling?"

Louise took a breath to calm herself. "It sounded like they were speaking Spanish. But how, without mouths?!"

"Without heads!" her friend shrieked back. The rest of the group tried to shush her.

"We need to get out of here," Bill stated the obvious, but the how was not so clear. "Look, let's take the railroad line," he pointed to the old cut that ran straight for three miles through the island to the port. "It's going to be the fastest way back to the boat."

"But what if one of those…"

"Or all three of those..."

"Or all three, come after us?"

Bill didn't have an answer. He looked at the other two men with him. They said nothing. It was getting dark and cold quick, and they needed to get to light and safety, to get their dates back to civilization. "We'll go through the woods as fast as we can. At least along the road, we probably will see them, the way they glow. Maybe we can outrun them."

One of the girls snorted. "I'll outrun them, outrun you, everyone." She had no intention of being caught by any strange ghosts on an empty island.

They made their way slowly at first to the trees lining the long road from the lighthouse. It was within only one mile of leaving the beach that they heard the first screeching yelps of their pursuers, and the horrendous headless pirates came out of the woods behind them.

Bill and his friends took off at a sprint. For half a mile, the ghosts gave chase, while the six humans huffed their way down the grassy road toward any promise of sanctuary and safety. They ducked into a tall stand of thick brush that scratched and poked at them. It was far better than the alternative.

With moments of silence that seemed to last all night, they waited. After about ten minutes, with the group no longer panting and tired, they began again to walk in the darkness of the trees back toward the little downtown where their boat was tied.

Again, after about a mile, the marauders made another appearance. They raised their cutlasses and ran, or flowed, toward the tired couples, who discovered newfound vigor after seeing the ghosts once again. This time they benefited not from a thicket of trees, but a few homes and roads that formed a more predictable maze. Again the ghosts disappeared, but all six knew they would be back.

"What do they want with us?" Louise was tired, out of breath, and scratched from the tree branches. A wisp of black hair fell over one of her soft brown eyes.

"They just seem to be mad," said Bill. "Look, you make a run for the boat, get it started," he pointed to the tall blond. "We will go that way. Let's see if they split up or who they chase."

With a quick nod, the blond and his date dashed toward the docks, while the four others headed toward the empty boardwalk.

It took only moments for the dreaded headless pirates to appear and run after Bill and his friends, leaving the blond man and his girl alone to bolt to the docks.

Through the small streets they ran, headless ghostly banshees screaming in muffled Spanish out of missing mouths as the pirates chased them through the roads and paths. Nearing exhaustion, Bill finally heard the cough and chug of a motor launch. "Quick, to the water!" he yelled.

They barely made it to a long dock when the boat pulled up alongside. Not waiting for it to stop, Bill threw Louise in as the other two jumped onto the deck. The pirates screamed as they found their way to the dark creosote decking. It was eerie as Bill turned back to see them one last time, the unintelligible screeching was loud, but their feet made no sound on the dock. The boat sped away into the dark night, aiming for channel markers and the warm lights of Southport on the other side of the Cape Fear river mouth.

"And that's pretty much it," Bill finished his tale, more with a shrug and a whimper than any attempt to make Benjamin Harper believe him.

No one was going to believe him.

"You don't believe me, do you?"

"On the contrary," said Parker, "I think your story has real merit. Do you know the ghost tales that have come from Smith Island?"

"No, I never heard much from there. Isn't there a woman that walks around Old Baldy? Something like that?"

Now it was Parker's turn to tell a story, but he felt he needed to be be brief. He didn't want Bill to think he was patronizing him.

"Do you know who Theodosia Burr was? No? She was the daughter of Aaron Burr, the third Vice President of the United States, and he famously killed Alexander Hamilton in a duel, while he was Vice President." Bill nodded, the story coming back to him.

"On the last day of 1812, with the war with Britain raging, she set sail from Charleston to go to New York to see her father, who had recently returned from exile of sorts. She dearly loved her father, and she wanted to see him one more time. See, she was likely dying of cancer by this time, and there was doubt she would even survive the trip. What she and no one else knew, was that they were right. She wouldn't, but it would not be cancer that turned the last screw. It would be pirates.

"Somewhere on Frying Pan Shoals, her sloop was stranded on the sandbars there. A group of Spanish pirates boarded the ship, killed the crew, but took Theodosia prisoner. She was taken to Smith Island. Faced with a short lifetime at the hands of the cutthroat pirates, Theodosia was emboldened to escape. When the three sailors left to guard her got drunk on the cheap rum they hid there, she saw her chance. She snuck away while they slept.

"But she soon discovered she was on an island, with nowhere to go, and no skills to survive on her own. She might have also sensed that she had little time left on earth. When the pirates awoke later that next day, and they discovered her missing, they grew both fearful and angry. They knew their captain would kill them for letting such a beautiful woman escape. So they chased after her, all across the island.

"They tracked her by her footprints, occasionally seeing her in the distance on the beach. But the pirates, hung over and in poor health themselves, could never catch up.

"Theodosia knew that this chase could not go on forever. She may have even seen the pirate sloop coming back toward Smith Island.

"It is said that, with her head held high, the last brave act she did was to walk into the breakers of the Atlantic, let her long white dress fill with salt water until it weighted her down, and she succumbed to the depths rather than give the filthy pirates their prize.

"Legend tells that the pirate captain was so mad that he cut the heads off of the guards right there on the beach, just left them in the sand."

Benjamin Parker cast a gaze at Bill, who was fascinated by the man's story. No longer in fear of disbelief, he almost didn't believe the story he heard. Except for the fact that the night before he had been chased by the very same pirates.

"It's thought that Theodosia still walks the beaches, partly in hopes of finding her way home, or maybe just to taunt the pirates who never caught her. Those fellows have been seen once or twice before, always chasing Theodosia, but never catching her."

"So why were they after us?"

"Who can tell?" Parker sighed. "The world is a different place with ghosts about. So what do you say? Can I tell your story? It sure is a good one."

Bill relented. It was a good story. And obviously it would already be getting around. "Might as well," he agreed.

It came out the next day. Bill read the article, and agreed it was a good story. Benjamin Parker had done a fine job of telling it, making Bill and his friends out to be brave heroes, when he knew he did little more than run. Well, he had tried to be brave in front of his girlfriend, Louise.

That thought led him to a bit of a surprise, when in the article there was a portrait of her printed with the story. He didn't think anyone would have photos of them, and it would have been more likely that he, Bill, would appear in the article than her.

He called up the newspaper to talk to Benjamin. "Thanks for writing such a good story about us," he began. "But where did you get that picture of Louise?"

"What picture?" Benjamin asked back.

"The one in the article, the girl with the short brown hair, that's my girlfriend, Louise, who was with me that night."

It was quiet on the other end of the phone. Then Benjamin spoke.

"That's not Louise," he said gravely. "That's a portrait of Theodosia Burr."

The Ghosts of Fort Fisher

Kure Beach

If I told you that Fort Fisher isn't haunted, would you believe me?

It seems like a strange question, I admit. You would think I would ask if you *would* believe it was haunted, not that it wasn't. "Do you believe Fort Fisher is haunted?" That seems like the correct question, right?

I stand by my first sentence.

Fort Fisher, the Gibraltar of the South, holds an important part of history for its role in the Civil War, when it protected the last bastion of connection to the world for the Confederate states during the Civil War. It was the protector of the blockade runners that flew swiftly through the Union naval siege just offshore. It was the greatest and last seacoast fort to fall.

Designed by Colonel William Lamb, a self taught engineer, the fort grew from a small seaside barricade with a few cannons to a giant sprawling edifice of guns and soldiers under his design. It truly seemed to be both immensely lethal and near impenetrable, a prickly porcupine that the Union feared to touch, as well as a chained but wild dog, measuring how far he could go to bite. Lamb personally had a hand in lengthening the chain. Upon assuming command, he ordered a cannon to be hastily taken out to the beach to skip a shot across the water in order to drive a Union gunboat out to sea. He also recovered the deadly accurate Whitworth rifles, vicious cannons with an intricate conical shot that would splinter the Union ships as they chased blockade runners into the Cape Fear.

It was without a doubt that Fort Fisher and the Union blockade were both at the tips of the two sharpest spears during the dark days of the Civil War.

Fort Fisher stood as a thorn in the side of the Union Navy for years, especially after an abortive attempt to take the fort failed in late 1864. General Braxton Bragg was recently reassigned to the area, much to the consternation of General William H. C. Whiting, as well as the rest of the entire Confederate armed forces. So hated and reviled was Bragg that upon his assignment to the Cape Fear that Virginia newspapers joked "Goodbye, Wilmington!" in their headlines. Little did they know how right they would be, and how deadly the events would become. Bragg thought erroneously that after the failed Christmas attack, the fort would be impenetrable, and when the next attack came, he did not send supporting troops.

General Whiting had a more dour opinion. He came to the fort when attack was imminent, stating to Col. Lamb,

"I'm here to share your fate, whatever that may be." Whiting knew that the full might of the Union would be thrown against the last bastion of the South, and he likely suspected the downfall of Fort Fisher was at hand, especially when General Bragg didn't send reinforcements during the second attack.

Whiting and Lamb would see an invasion to the fort that would be one of the bloodiest death scenes of the entire war. Both General Whiting and Colonel Lamb would be wounded as they personally lead defenses. The battles broke down into such harsh conditions that rifle butts and knives were used as much as Minié balls and cannon shot. The battle left Colonel Lamb with over 550 dead, one of the highest percentages of loss from any battle in the Civil War. Whiting would go down with two shots in his leg. He was captured, but due to his wound, as well as ongoing illnesses, and ultimately the onset of dysentery, he would die while imprisoned.

The battle would define the end of the war, but it seems to have led on into present day, at least by some accounts. In the years after the battle up to present day, the entirety of Fort Fisher has been a place of mystery and eeriness. The tall twisted oaks that grow up just inside the beach now cast strange shadows in the eveningtime, where the branches, reaching out like long bony fingers of death, shade mysterious specters within their midst. Soldiers are heard moving in the woods to this day, even when the rest of the island is silent and calm. The distant sounds of battle, explosions, the sounds of horses' hooves delivering a muffled pounding to the loamy sand, all have been heard in the background of Fort Fisher.

As the sun sets, a lone figure has been seen walking the parapets. It is a figure in gray, in more ways than one.

Many speculate that it is General Whiting himself, who came to the fort to help in its defense, not just to lead with command, but to lead with example. Whiting believed, even in prison as he lay suffering and dying, that the fort fell solely due to General Bragg's failure to command. It is thought that Whiting is still walking the parapets, on guard for an attack that will never come again, in hopes of changing a history that already happened.

But now, I go back to my original question. Remember it? If I told you Fort Fisher isn't haunted, would you believe me? Now, after hearing the story, even in its most basic, simplistic form, and knowing there was so much carnage, so much horrible death, as well as a mountain of regret and anger bigger than any fort wall, well, how could you not believe the fort was haunted? Especially after reading that so many people have seen the ghosts, heard them, even seen the marks they leave and imprints that remain.

Well, it still might be so, that Fort Fisher is not actually haunted.

Considering all the events that have been seen and heard across the land that is Fort Fisher, it may have a different cause to the supposed haunting. Some paranormal investigators have theorized that the ghosts that have been seen or heard are actually past events encroaching on present day. The battle of Fort Fisher was so ferocious, so vicious, that the land itself remembers the scars and pain of the soldiers on it. Confederate soldiers, many conscripts or lesser trained, put up a fight far past their breaking point, as many, more than a quarter of the entire fort, were wounded or died. The Union soldiers took even worse numbers on a larger force. Both knew they were fighting against an enemy they could have known in peaceful times, not some nameless faceless invader. The tragedy that occurred and the malice toward one another was an artificial trigger pulled when the battle got real and friends saw friends dying beside them.

So it is very well possible that the sounds and feelings felt at Fort Fisher aren't those of ghosts still remaining today, but the remnants of another day, ghosts of a different time, possibly.

One of the many tales of haunts seen along Fort Fisher is that of soldiers standing in the trees, waiting for the inevitable attack from the north, where the Union army would be coming. The soldiers still await the attack, hoping that the cannons that were damaged or destroyed, the mines buried underground waiting for their own chance to spill

blood, and even their own rifles can somehow find a way to send forth death. It's a jarring thought, just how aware they must have been of how bad things would be, whatever fate made it out for them. It is therefor something not to be taken lightly that the history of all the pain may not be able to hold itself back from times long ago.

But now, the dogs of war that once hunted here have long ago turned into ghost hounds, digging the bones of the dead that have long turned to dust.

Perhaps one day, the land, and the ghosts if they are there, will find peace.

Dunbar Davis

Oak Island

Ghosts can stick around for the strangest of reasons. There s a mythos to the ghost mystique that says a spirit remains when there is unfinished business, or perhaps the person doesn't know they have passed on. Sometimes it is a punishment, others almost a reward. They just like where they are, so they remain. It could be a sense of duty, or a promise to keep.

Dunbar Davis may just be an outlier in all these choices.

As a ghost, he's not really much. He is almost a problem when it comes to ghost stories, actually. There is not very much to report. Sometimes ghosts are like that. You'll see.

But as a person, he had quite a story. Maybe four stories. Well, actually, a lot more, but four stories come to mind.

Dunbar Davis held the enviable job of being a keeper of the Lifesaving Service that worked along the coast of Oak Island before the turn of the twentieth century. It was the type of job that was very easy right up until it became incredibly hard. A Lifesaver had to be ready to run to the beach to rescue the crews of sinking, broken ships, and if the ships were too far out in the ocean, the Lifesaving crew would go out in long boats to take the stranded sailors from their ships, even as wind, rain, and waves pounded both sailor and rescuer into a salty pulp. A rescue was hard, hard work. It was not a job for the weak; no one who did the work of a Lifesaver would ever worry about being labeled a coward.

The Lifesaving Service was created as a precursor to the US Coast Guard, as sailing ships were at risk from the unpredictable storms and uncharted coasts where the tall masted ships plied the churning rough waves of an unpredictable Atlantic Ocean during the rough winter and spring storms.

But that was one of the benefits to the job of a lifesaver; it was somewhat part time. Once the spring storms abated, travel across the Atlantic from the Caribbean to New York and back again was considered to be relatively safe. Outside of the risk of hurricanes, which were unpredictable beasts especially in the 1800s, summer was a peaceful time for the Lifesaving Service. So much so that the crews were given the summer off. From the end of April to the end of August, the only person kept on station was the Keeper.

In this case it was Dunbar Davis.

Dunbar enjoyed his summer off. Being a family man, he was able to travel to Southport and farther to Wilmington on occasion. His family and the lighthouse keeper's own brood on nearby Smith Island would often spend time together. The Atlantic Ocean was supplied with water so warm from the Gulf Stream that it felt like a bath tub, or soup, as he and his family would swim in the shore. The long days and late sunset would allow for days full of fishing or crabbing, almost outside the back door of the Lifesaver's station. The only issue was that Dunbar Davis was still technically on call, and couldn't go away for anything more than a day or evening. Even though nothing would ever, ever happen in the summer months, especially the end days of August. The only thing Dunbar Davis had to do was prepare the station for the influx of his crew on September 1st, 1893.

Unfortunately for him and many others, the warm Atlantic waters and the thick hot air of the Cape Verde Islands had other plans not known to anyone along the US coast. A hurricane was brewing up on August 17th. It would follow a track north of Haiti, then just outside of Cuba, as if it knew all along where it was going. The gentle arc and fast pace of the hurricane led it straight for Charleston, SC, and the vulnerable Carolina Coast.

At the time there was no way of predictions for hurricanes, and communication was decidedly lacking, to the point that all news was old news. Ships would founder and fail in the huge storm as they were caught off guard by the wind and waves. Eight ships perished in the hurricane that also killed hundreds on the South Carolina shore. Eight ships that were lost completely, upturned and sunk, with their crews all unwilling sacrifices to a watery, lost grave.

As unfortunate as the storm would be, there was also good fortune for many, and that fortune would come from Dunbar Davis, the man who stood watch on August 27th, during the easy time, when the storms weren't supposed to come, when the seas weren't supposed to be rough. It would be no easy day for Dunbar Davis. It would, in fact, be no easy set of several days. And it would begin just after midnight on August 27, 1893.

The schooner *Three Sisters* would be caught in the dregs of the storm, just off Frying Pan Shoals, notorious for its shallow sand bars that would reach up for a ship's hull to grab and break. In this case, the hurricane did more damage as great waves washed both the captain and first mate overboard to a watery doom. The ship was now left to the charge of the cook, who commanded a five man crew. Unskilled in piloting nor navigation, the cook thought it would be best to strand the *Three Sisters* on the beach just north of Smiths Island, not knowing that this would be the worst possible thing to do, as the ship would surely crack up, spilling contents and crew into the unforgiving ocean to drown and be lost.

At the time, the first bit of good fortune came to the crew not from Davis, but from his partner at the Cape Fear Station on Smith Island, John Watts. Keeper Watts spotted the ship in distress and was able to signal to them to anchor offshore, and that a rescue could be more easily made from that point.

That was the easy part.

Dunbar Davis had just begun the hard part, which would last much longer than he, or his stomach, would predict. Having seen the masts of the ship at sea from his point on Oak Island, he rowed across the mouth of the Cape Fear, only to meet with Keeper Watts passing the other way.

In the churning waters, the two discussed a plan where Davis would prepare his surf boat for rescue while Watts continued to Southport for volunteers. The regular lifesaving crew was not even on the island yet.

By 8:30 that night, Dunbar, Watts, and nine volunteers began the long row across the mouth of the Cape Fear River, which still churned with the waves from the hurricane. It would not be until the next day, around 1:00 a.m., that the volunteer crew would even make it to the Oak Island station, where they rested for a few hours before moving on before dawn to save the crew of the *Thee Sisters*.

By sunrise they had reached the anchored vessel, after an hour-long row across the point of Bald Head Island. The rescue was possibly the easiest part of the entire incident. The crew of the *Three Sisters* was taken to Southport for much needed care from the beating they had taken from the hurricane. August 28th, 1893 ended before Davis could get home, though he had gotten the sailors to a safe place.

But at least the job was done. Dunbar Davis had done his duty, along with several other brave volunteers. It had been a long full day, and more than a day since Dunbar Davis had eaten or slept, but such was the life of a Lifesaver. Soon he could cross back over to Oak Island, to enjoy a hot meal lovingly prepared by his dutiful wife, and then a long rest in his bed.

When he got within sight of the Lifesaving Station at Oak Island, he knew this was not going to happen. The warning signal of a ship in distress was flying on the pole atop the building.

Davis had barely gotten home when he was told by his wife, who had also run up the flag, that the ship *Wustrow* was in distress. It was stranded nine miles west, in the opposite direction from which he had just come. It had stranded on a sandbar and had broken up in the waves. Davis climbed his watchtower to see if he could spy the ship or its remains. Locals had alerted him that while the ship was now in splinters, the crew had made it ashore and were in the care of fishermen nearby. Davis had long ago sent the original volunteers back home from the *Three Sisters* rescue. He had gathered a few back in case they were needed, but with the news of the crew of the *Wustrow* being saved, he planned to tell them to go home, too. But when he climbed the tower, he spotted the ship still intact. A moment of relief was replaced with dread. The *Wustrow* had been a brig, with two tall masts. This ship was a three mast schooner.

He now knew that not one, but two ships were now aground to the west of Oak Island.

Gathering his volunteers, they attempted to row out and do another sea rescue, but the onshore push of waves was too brutal for the crew and little surfboat. It would be another long day for Dunbar Davis.

He gathered the supplies needed for a shore rescue, which included a Lyle Gun and breeches buoy. The small cannon would be anchored in the sand, then fire a small projectile with a rope out to the high masts of the stranded ship. The crew would pull the rope to them, bringing a heavier line that would be secured to the highest spot on a mast. Then the shipwrecked crew would sit one at a time in the breeches buoy, a round rescue device with stirrups that would be pulled over the long line across the breaking waves to shore. It was neither graceful nor comfortable, as the sailors would often get dipped into the sea before touching land, but in their predicament, they surely wouldn't care.

The issue that Dunbar Davis had was that the wreck was nine miles away, over storm soaked sand that had been cut by numerous overwashes and miniature inlets. It was the middle of the afternoon, which Davis could only tell by his watch as the sky was overcast, covered with dark gray scudding clouds filled with rain. He and his crew had only just set out on their next rescue. Dunbar Davis felt his stomach growl and churn from lack of food.

The cart hauling the supplies continually stuck in the beach. The going was difficult, sometimes near impossible. He measured his progress in yards, sometimes inches. Davis attempted to lighten the cart by removing precious tools. Fortune smiled upon him as a man with a mule was employed to drag the stubborn cart to where the *Wustrow* had broken. The schooner, the *Kate E. Gifford*, had attempted to make way but had stranded herself on the sandbar. By now the sun was setting. He left a volunteer at the beach across from the stranded schooner to build a fire. It was both a comforting marker and a promise that they would attempt a rescue as soon as possible. Davis had to go back for the rest of his equipment first.

It seemed like no good luck would come to him. The rain lashed at the face of Dunbar Davis. He had not eaten in over a day, and even with the rain pelting him, had not had a drink of water in hours. He was sore and tired, as well as scratched and bloody from his travails and the earlier rescue of the *Three Sisters*. The day was over, and night was setting in, but nothing was over for Dunbar Davis.

Thanks to the help of a local with a team of oxen, the rest of the rescue apparatus was slowly moved from where it lay to where it needed to be, on the beach where the *Gifford* sat just offshore. It was now 2 a.m. on August 30th.

Dunbar Davis and his volunteer crew couldn't see the *Gifford* in the darkness, except for the few burning lights that marked the bare outlines of the ship. Davis was tired, with the darkness bringing on a worsening exhaustion that was exacerbated by the blowing sand and lashing rain. With a strength and diligence that few would find, Davis and his dedicated volunteers dug in a sand anchor and set up the Lyle gun. They fired into the darkness, but knew the rope flew straight and true to where the *Gifford* hid. The line hung above the water in a long arc, not drifting in the sea loose.

The darkness held a problem, though. None of the tired sailors aboard the *Gifford* could see the rope to make it tight. Davis sat on the beach, snuggled up in a cold and wet coat by a beach fire to wait until morning for the crew to spot the rope and secure it to the mast.

By dawn on August 30th, the sailors from the *Gifford* finally awoke to find their rescue draped over the crosstrees above them. Good fortune mixed with bad. Their rescue was imminent, but the *Gifford* was breaking apart under them. One by one the crew were loaded into the breeches buoy and transferred from the ship to the waiting beach. What was a wet, sandy, and miserable spot to spend a night for Davis was a blessing to the crew of the *Gifford*.

By now it was the afternoon of August 30th, 1893. Dunbar Davis sent the rescued crew members on the slow walk of nine miles back to the lifesaving station for food and shelter. The empty building, missing the soon to return Lifesaving crew, would be filled with sailors. Davis did a count in his head, hoping his fuzzy brain, lacking sleep and food, could calculate and remember all that had happened in the past few days. The *Three Sisters*, stranded but salvageable, with five members of the crew saved and safe.

The *Wustrow*, broken apart with most of the cargo lost but a crew of nine safely on land. And now the *Kate E. Gifford*, turning to splinters as he watched, but the crew now on their way to hot food and dry beds. As miserable as he felt, it had been a good day.

Through the mush that was his thoughts, he realized it had been almost three days. At least it was over, he thought. In his mind he could taste his wife's cooking, something hot, thick, filling. Chicken and dumplings, maybe, or perhaps sausage fried in a pan with buttered vegetables, and soft bread with a chewy crust. And then a bed, soft, so soft… All the sheets had been cleaned and folded for the upcoming crew, they would be white, smooth, … soft… Davis felt himself dozing in the afternoon sun that had finally appeared after four days of gloom.

The beach fire was built up so that Davis and one member of the rescued sailors could stay at the water's edge to guard the crates washed out of the broken ship onto the shore. They would take turns sleeping.

But sleep wasn't allowed just yet.

In the twilight, Davis spotted movement outside of the breakers. A jolly-boat from a ship somewhere out on the Atlantic was rowing into shore.

Tired but on duty, Davis and the faithful steward of the *Gifford* ran into the waves to help pull the rowboat ashore. Seven men were aboard. The boat was from the schooner *Jennie E. Thomas*. That ship had become unmanageable, waterlogged and heavy in the churning waves, with all food and water either exhausted or tainted by the salt water. Four crew members used the jolly-boat to row to a nearby ship, the *Enchantress*, to get supplies, but that ship was in even worse condition. It was drifting toward shore with an injured captain and lost a mate that had been washed overboard and drowned. The captain of the *Enchantress* and two crew members boarded the jolly-boat and they rowed toward the only light they saw, the fire on the beach where Dunbar Davis warmed his hungry body.

The rescued sailors had been without food for longer than he had, Davis realized. He sent them to his station for food and care as well.

Finally, Dunbar Davis found his work to be done. He hired a man to guard the supplies, his Lyle gun, the wagon, the beaten jolly-boat, and began his own long walk back to the station, his home. On his walk he added the seven men in the jolly-boat to his count of sailors rescued since he had left home on August 27th. It had been a long day, but a good one.

When he finally got to his quarters, Davis was starving. His throat was parched and dry on the inside, but his clothes and body were soaked with rain, coated with sand, weaved with seaweed. He was close to home, close to food and water, and close to sleep. It wouldn't be long now.

Unfortunately, the long day wasn't quite over. The quarters were overrun by stranded sailors, all as starving and injured as he was. The sailors from the *Wustrow* wore the clothes of the lifesavers; theirs had been torn to shreds in the wreck and had arrived almost naked. Davis' wife had quickly directed them to clean clothes before cooking all the food in the quarters for the hungry sailors. When Dunbar Davis finally arrived, all the food in the house had been eaten. Not a morsel remained.

This time, goof fortune relieved the bad, when the lighthouse keeper and his wife arrived with large amounts of hot food, water, tea, coffee, whatever they could carry. Davis finally satisfied his hunger, and began to look for a bed.

But all the beds were taken. In a house meant to hold and entire crew of lifesavers, there was not a place to rest his body. All the beds were occupied, including his own. Davis didn't really care. He knew what the storm-lashed sailors had been through. He was so tired, he could sleep anywhere. His wife was able to move one sailor out of a small room upstairs. She pulled out one of those clean white sheets that Davis dreamed about. He fell into a comfortable, deep sleep.

He would need the rest. The next day was September 1st, 1893. That was when the seasonal lifesaving crew would show up at the station. It would be his first day of work. When the storms would finally come to Oak Island.

Now, this would be a great tale on its own, but this *is* a ghost story. Dunbar Davis would wake up sometime the next day and go back to work. He would continue to work, living another thirty years, passing on in 1923 after living a good life, a hero's life. The old keeper's station would be saved, moved, and turned into a private home. And of course, it would be haunted by Dunbar Davis.

It's the usual haunting, nothing spectacular. Footsteps are heard walking upstairs when no one is on the upper floor. Items occasionally move. A door to a bedroom won't stay closed even when it is shut tight. There isn't much story there, especially when compared to a day or three in the life of Dunbar Davis, keeper of the Oak Island Lifesaving Station, and hero of the rescue of five ships in one day, the *Three Sisters*, the *Wustrow*, the *Kate E. Gifford*, the *Jennie E. Thomas*, and the *Enchantress*.

So why does Dunbar Davis still haunt his old home? At the beginning of this tale, there were the ideas of why spirits stay where they are. Davis had no unfinished business; he instead had completed his tasks. He had no undue punishments in his life; he remains a heroic figure. Then why does he still haunt the keeper's quarters?

The answer is simple. He's still trying to catch up on his sleep!

Afterword

Ending with the tale of Dunbar Davis, hero of the Lifesaving Corps, but only a vague and unimpressive ghost, is somewhat apropos for this book. And I'll tell you why.

Wilmington is full of ghosts and ghost stories. When I wrote my other books in this collection, I actually had a hard time finding enough stories to tell. I needed them to be fun, scary, historical, important, entertaining, all that which makes a ghost tale memorable. I was able to find a lot of ghost stories, certainly. But an actual ghost *tale*? That's a little different.

See, some of these ghost legends are simplistic. They simply say that a ghost exists. There's nothing more to the story. There may even be less to the story than the legend, like it could be that the ghost isn't even a ghost. It's all made up. I have an inside joke for these types of ghost stories. I call them Lawnmower Man ghosts.

When I did my research for haunted places in North Carolina for *Did You See That Ghost?* I found one such tale that gave rise to the name. I was looking everywhere, as I am often to do, in search of the best and strangest legends, not just the usual fare for you, my dear readers. Sometimes I get deep into rabbit holes and find some really weird stuff, though. This one tale was just such a trap for me. I found this ghost story, out of Columbia, a small town on the way to and from the Outer Banks that most people only know from the rest area there. The legend was, and I will try to tell it in the vernacular of the spirit of the legend, that there was this guy, he lived in a trailer over behind the gas station. He died, and if you go over to his trailer in the woods, he comes out on a riding lawnmower and chases you.

And that's it.

I mean… that's it?

It's a great story, stupid, funny, completely unbelievable, but just great. Who ever heard of a ghost chasing you down on a riding lawnmower?! No explanation of who he was, why he died, why the heck he chases you on a riding lawnmower, nothing. Seriously, it could just be a guy on a riding lawnmower that chases you. How would we even know he's a ghost? Like you're going to get close to him and poke your finger through him?

So, that's the lawnmower man ghost.

And that was kind of the problem I had with a lot of the ghosts from Wilmington and around there. Like I mentioned in the story of Dunbar Davis, there's just not a lot there as a ghost story.

What was surprising was that, even though there were a lot of ghost stories in Wilmington, there wasn't enough to really write a book that would be entertaining and informative. When I started this whole series, I wanted to deliver stories that weren't in every other collection of ghost books, and I had to keep up my end of the bargain with this book.

One of the big ones that is missing here is of course the *USS North Carolina*. It's one of the most well known haunts in the area. The story is that there may be two ghosts there, one who is a bit of a prankster, a young blond man, and another is a more angry spirit. But the issue is, no one really knows who they were. They are suspected of being two members of the six who perished in a torpedo strike on the ship. One of the interesting things about the *North*

Carolina is that very few people lost their lives on the ship, and more were from accidents than enemy attacks. I looked up the six who died in the torpedo attack, and none seemed to be a young blond man, nor fit the even more vague description of the other ghost. There just was no story there. I couldn't do them the proper honor they need to tell a legend, and I just couldn't make it all up. So that's why it's not in there.

There are several bars and shops throughout the downtown area that report hauntings. Some are really interesting. But again, a ghost that comes by to drink a beer doesn't have much of a story. I could tell you a story about my brother coming by to drink a beer and it would be more interesting.

Another really famous ghost for the area is the Gray Man of Oak Island. The legend of the Gray Man is that he shows up before a hurricane as a warning of the danger to come. The trouble is, outside of that being the bulk of the tale, I already told the story with the Gray Man of Hatteras. I wasn't going to redo a story for you. Y'all gotta get your money's worth, right?

And in that same vein, I already did the story of Samuel Jocelyn, the legend of him being buried alive at St. James Episcopal Church. It's a story from *In The Shadows Of The Pines*, and it's a great version of the legend, not one most have heard before. I highly recommend reading it.

So, yes, I left a few out. But I also really delivered on a lot of great tales. I found some legends and unique versions of these stories that haven't been heard before. The Hanging Tree is a fun take on a rather morbid and sensitive topic, and yes, the tree really is there. The legend of Theodosia Burr, a figure that has been attached to many places from South Carolina all the way to Nags Head, is well known, but the headless Spanish pirates, that's a story that isn't really shared. And, while I can't say it really happened, I did actually find a newspaper article from that year that described the very events in the story. I changed the names and embellished the story, or course. Remember, I always say, "It's a ghost *story*!" It needs to be fun, spooky, entertaining. The tale has to make people not notice the campfire going out until the telling is over.

The Maco Light tale is a good example. That is a story that has been told by everyone, it's such a prevalent legend because the light was so real, so many saw it. But, yes, the legend was made up. There was no Joe Baldwin. But there really was a Charles Baldwin who lost his life and his body.

The same with Tony the Ghost in Southport. The legend says he died before his first night performing, but newspaper articles say it was near the end of the summer. He really is buried in Southport, leaving a family behind.

So, yes, these are fun, spooky, scary ghost stories. They also have truth behind them. And history. Wilmington and the Cape Fear, all the way to the coast, in Wrightsville and Carolina Beach, down to the fort and beyond, through the marshlands, all the little towns and beachfront homes, there's a lot of stories to tell and to hear. I hope that you, my dear readers, will find something to love, maybe a little something to chill your blood, or something to make you want to learn more. I know this book isn't really like my fun offbeat travel books, but still, it's a great place to start your exploring. There is so much to discover. Who knows, maybe you can find the next story, and tell it to me!

About the Author

Joe Sledge is the author of his *Did You See That?* series of travel books, as well as his Haunting North Carolina collection of ghost tales in this series. He also has written two fiction novels, with more on the way.

Inspired by finding an old copy of *Nag's Head*, a book written in the mid 1800s about vacation life on the coast, he republished that book, as well as later republishing *Kinnakeet Adventure*, by Stanley Green, who turned out to be a distant great great uncle of sorts.

Joe is from the Outer Banks, where ghost stories were the regular fare for entertainment on beach house porches and dark beach shorelines as he grew up. He attended UNC Chapel Hill, and traveled extensively when he was not working as a teacher. He currently writes and runs his publishing company, Gravity Well Books. When not writing, he enjoys spending time with his family. When he *is* writing, he would prefer to be spending time with his family as well.